Yard Dog Press
710 W. Redbud Lane
Alma, AR 72921-7247

http://www.yarddogpress.com

I0652919

Edited by Selina Rosen
Copy Editor & Technical Editor Lynn Rosen
Cover & title page art by Sherri Dean
Back cover art by James Hollaman

First Edition June 15, 2016
Printed in the United States of America
0 9 8 7 6 5 4 3 2 1

Flush Fiction, Volume II:

Twenty Years of Letting It Go!

Edited by Selina Rosen

Sherri Dean did the cover art for the first *Flush Fiction,* and has long referred to herself in the third person, the "royal we," if you will, as the Queen of the Flying Monkeys. She has recently earned the title of The Feisty Mistress of Fear. (If you've met her you already know. If not, do so and BUY HER STUFF!) In addition to commanding her monkey minions she likes shiny presents and hearing from fans on Facebook, Twitter and the upcoming website. Now, go forth and make with the monkey adoration! She needs praise; lie if you must. (See her full bio after the last story.)

Flush Fiction, Volume II: Twenty Years of Letting It Go!
Edited by Selina Rosen
First Edition Copyright © 2016
Published by Yard Dog Press

ISBN 978-1-937105-82-2
Flush Fiction, Volume II: Twenty Years of Letting It Go!
First Edition Copyright by Yard Dog Press
Foreword, © 2006 Selina Rosen, edited for this edition
"The Minimum Wages of Sin," James K. Burk
"Ninefold Appearances," Paul Carlson
"Colonel Starbreaker Makes A House Call," Richard Dansky
"'Til Death Us Do Part," Christopher Donahue
"Killer Kudzu," James Dorr
"Hello, I Am the Antichrist," Phillip Drayer Duncan
"An Unconventional Death," Rhonda Eudaly
"Wainscoting's Folly," Tim Frayser
"My Addiction," James Hollaman
"Princess in Boots," Trina Jacobs
"Dark Noise," vickey malone kennedy
"The Troll in Tower Grove Park," Zoanne Leavy
"Salvage," William Ledbetter
"High Noon Zombies," John Moore
"Roll for Initiative," Tracy S. Morris
"Bloodsucking Monkeys," Ethan Nahté
"Destination: Uranus," Jody Lynn Nye
"The Way of the Jedy," Gloria Oliver
"Dark Matter Degree," Morris Reban
"Greeter By Day—Skeeters By Night," Selina Rosen
"Stranded at the Gates of Hell," Susan Satterfield
"A Dark Bird," Bradley H. Sinor
"Crocaroo," Sue Sinor
"Field Test No. 421," Allison Stein
"Confessions of A Husband Beater," Katherine A. Turski, first appeared in
    Uncle John's Bathroom Reader Presents Flush Fiction, Portable Press, 2012
"Cougar," Laura J. Underwood
"Aide De Tramp," © Mel. White, 2016

Table of Contents

Foreword

So... some of you are no doubt asking yourself about now, "What are the ground-breaking talented agents of the Yard Dog Press empire doing now and just what is this, *Flush Fiction*?" The rest of you are all asking yourselves, "What the fuck are those morons at Yard Dog doing now and what the hell is this *Flush Fiction*?"

Allow me to explain... *Flush Fiction* is a true indicator of just what we are and what we're trying to do at Yard Dog Press. A bunch of us were sitting around at my house for our yearly party which we call ConDome—we are nothing if not dripping with class—I was discussing the inability of some authors to gauge how long it will take them to read one of their stories. This had become a problem because of the Yard Dog Press traveling Road Show... Don't know what that is?

The Yard Dog press traveling Road Show is something that we as a group do at any convention that will allow it. You see we had noticed that readings were becoming increasingly poorly attended; in order for a reading to be successful you need to have an audience. So Bill Allen and I were talking about how to do this and I said I thought we'd do better if several authors were at one reading and all did short funny stuff, that's when Bill came up with the Road show idea, we could do readings and acts and maybe some stand up. Turn it into more of a show and then more people would come. And then one of those moments of pure genius happened. Just before we were supposed to do the very first road show—the night before in fact—we all went to a reading Melanie Fletcher was doing, and behind her just for fun Sherri Dean started to do a pantomime of everything Mel was reading and by the time the road show took the stage it had become a show, where one of the writers would read and other writers and artists would do an interpretive dance to what they were reading. This became highly successful and packed the house until they started to give us bigger and bigger rooms and more and more time.

Now back to the problem that arose because of the road shows. I would tell the writers that they had five minutes to read and they would read for ten or fifteen minutes thus running one hour shows into two hour shows and two hour shows into three and some writers still didn't get to read. I was discussing my idea for a solution at ConDome. I had decided that we needed to put together a book of flash fiction showcasing all our writers and giving them a piece that they could read in five minutes or less. We decided the pieces should be funny, but didn't have to be, they should be fairly visual so that the interpretive dancers had something to do, they had to be under a thousand words, and they had to be complete stories, no vignettes. After several minutes of discussion someone said, "Just the right length for reading on the can." Then Matt Reiten screams out, *Flush Fiction!* We should call it *Flush Fiction.*

"Genius!" I proclaimed. "Stories to be read in one sitting." Brilliant idea.

Much later as I started to write out the guidelines I realized we had a huge problem. There would be dozens of writers in this collection, so the royalty statements all by themselves would be a nightmare. Then by the time you split the money that many ways we'd be writing checks for twenty cents; this wasn't an option. But being a professional writer myself I don't believe in writers giving away their work, so the next question became how do I make this worthwhile to everyone and still make it feasible? The answer came when one of our writers had a health scare. This isn't the first time this has happened, and it won't be the last, but here's the thing: most of our writers either have no health benefits or have them but would still be screwed if they got sick because it wouldn't cover everything. And guess what? They aren't rich. So it was decided that we would put seventy-five percent of the profits (after cost of printing) from *Flush Fiction* into a health fund that could be used to help out our writers and artists if they needed it, and we'd keep the other twenty-five percent to help cover overhead costs for this and other titles.

So *Flush Fiction* is not just a showcase of many of our very-talented writers and artists, but it is also a testament to what we truly are: a community of artists bound together by our art and our need to entertain our clientele. If I stayed in my own head and didn't listen to and watch the writers and artists, Yard Dog Press would be just like every other house—a business with no soul. Instead, it's a vital, living entity with a personality all its own. Yard Dog Press is not an extension of me; it is the ideas of everyone who works for it. When you buy a Yard Dog Press book, you aren't just supplying yourself with some great inexpensive entertainment, you're also helping to preserve a style of writing science fiction (I'm from the old school where Science fiction meant horror and fantasy too without having to say all three every time) which is sadly harder and harder to find on bookstore shelves. You aren't just supporting my dream to bring our sort of Sci Fi back to the readers, but you're supporting the dreams and hopes of every writer and artist who works for us, a dream that there is still a place for our work in the hearts of science fiction fans and readers in general.

I edited *Flush Fiction*, but I held to my promise not to reject anything. I have always contended that a writer writes their best work when they write just exactly what they want to write without worrying about what any editor, agent or publisher has to say. I think the stories in *Flush Fiction* prove my point; there isn't a dog in the bunch. Creative people are always being told that they need to have their hands tied to do better work. I was told by one big-shot editor from a New York house, "You're a good writer, but what you need is for an agent to stick you in a box and tell you what to write." If a writer can't write what they want, they might as well be digging ditch. At least then they can be sure of a pay check.

Now some of the biggest names in this business make their livings writing seven-hundred-thousand word vignettes. They wouldn't know how to tell a complete story if it jumped up and bit them on the ass, so keep that in mind as you read the stories in *Flush Fiction*. None of these stories are over three thousand words, and most are under one thousand. Yet every one of them is a complete story, with a beginning a middle and an end that's conclusive. If a certain rich and famous writer (who shall remain nameless) can't finish a story in several extremely-long books, how genius are these fuckers that can do it in under a thousand words.

The Minimum Wages of Sin
James K. Burk

Sneg wiped the bloody sweat from his forehead with a scaly arm then reached for the paper that had appeared in his in-box. He scanned the sheet, a memo from his supervisor to be in the supervisor's office in three minutes. As he finished reading, the paper burst into flames, singeing his fingers. He cursed, stuck his fingers in his mouth, and waved his hand.

Dashing to the escalator, he ran until he was panting like a steam engine going up a steep grade. In Hell, of course, all the escalators ran only down and his boss's office was three floors above. His fingers convulsed at the memory of the request he'd submitted for up escalators. That had required him to fill out six hundred sixty-six forms, all in triplicate. The request had, of course, been denied.

As he frantically wheezed his way up the down escalator he cursed again. Hell, the largest and most lethargic bureaucracy in the universe, filled each office with grim-faced pencil-pushers, every one of whom hated his/her job.

Reaching the right floor, he dashed down the ridiculously long corridor and, with the last of his breath, flung himself through the door of Stog's office.

Stog glared at him. "You're seventeen seconds late. I have to cancel your weekend off and dock you a day's pay."

Sneg suppressed a sob. After over six hundred years, he'd felt he was entitled to a weekend off. He composed himself, realizing that hope existed in Hell as a special punishment, as hopes existed only to be dashed.

"Actually," Stog said, "I'm to offer you a commendation. As you know, we actually have a very easy job—to corrupt humans. As you also know, it's a ludicrously simple job, as no more corruptible a species has ever been created."

He pushed a button on his desk and a screen slid down from the ceiling. "We've been keeping research busy for centuries trying to invent a new, improved form of sin. The closest we've come was the result of observing human politicians, who have reached levels of dishonesty we have only begun to fathom. Not new, but definitely improved."

"But you, Sneg, have brought one of the seven deadly sins to a group who seemed to be immune. Some of the trailer park denizens seemed incapable of lust. Lust is about more than sex. There's the anticipation, the time spent imagining, all the extra touches. Since those people were forever screwing anything that breathed—and they weren't always even fanatical about that—they didn't experience true lust."

Pictures, some of them still shots, some videos, began to play on the screen. After a moment's horrid fascination, Sneg put his hands over his eyes. After (he hoped) the stream of images, most of which wanted to make him pour bleach into his eyes, abated he lowered a finger and took a peak with one eye and saw what appeared to be carnal knowledge of roadkill. He shuddered and firmly closed both eyes. He waited until Stog said, "Okay, you can look now."

The darkened screen was a great improvement.

"You, however, did manage to find a way to bring lust to that trailer park."

The screen showed a bloated face, eyes glassy, apparently staring at something which had aroused its owner. The view shifted to what had caused the lust—a gleaming row of brand new pickups, with tires and wheels the size of an inflatable pool and so jacked up they would require a ladder to get to the door. The scene changed to the human, eyes half closed, sitting in the cab of a pickup. His hands caressed and stroked the dashboard and the leather seats and he was obviously in the throes of ecstasy.

"You not only brought lust to them by setting up the car lot with pickups but dishonesty and frustration has increased by three hundred percent, as they find out what the dealer is charging and lying on the loan applications. Very well done, Sneg, very well done. So the boss has ordered me to present you this commendation."

Stog drew out a medal about the size of an ashtray and as gaudy as a carny van. "It'll only hurt a little bit," he said, as he pinned it to Sneg's chest. Since Sneg didn't wear a shirt it hurt like Hell, but Sneg had known it would be a lie.

"And in honor of this special occasion, your request has been granted—for the next five minutes. For those five minutes, all Hell's escalators will be up escalators. I want you back in your office in three minutes. Go."

James K. Burk is an odd duck. In fact, one of his favorite punchlines is "Dey bet on de duck." His past is so checkered it's almost plaid. One of his favorite jobs was being a Sunday gunman at an amusement park where he fell off roofs, over hitching posts, out of wagons, and into horse troughs. Sometimes it was even intentional. Often exhibiting the attention span of a chipmunk on caffeine, he's followed half a hundred odd passions.

He is to writing what a left-handed swordsman is to fencing. He sees different openings and exploits different approaches. Some of the oddity is expressed in a strange, lurking sense of humor which turns up in odd places.

He takes pride in being distinctive and he has a weakness for writers' challenges. He refuses to limit himself to any genres. Along with fantasy, science fiction, weird westerns, and action/ adventure, he has written reviews, criticism, and even some non-fiction

Bibliography:
High Rage (Fantasy)
Taking Hope (Fantasy)
Home Is the Hunter (Science Fiction, half of Double Dog #3)
The Twelve (Fantasy)
Redemption (Science Fiction)
Mirror, Mirror, And Other Reflections (Fantasy Shorts)
The Ghoul of Socorro (Novella, Weird Western, Book 4 of the
    Night Marshal series)
Numerous Short Stories in chapbooks and anthologies.

Ninefold Appearances
Paul Carlson

Muscles bulging, sword dark with blood, the brave warrior cut a swath through his enemy's ranks. Each morning, mighty Lament would pause to grant healing to his companions. Even so, he never forgot that the realm depended upon his might alone, one man to protect them from evil foes. Tireless, legendary, enemies did indeed lament crossing his path.

Serious yet frustrated, two white-clad doctors stood beside the patient's bed. First they tested the restraints on his twitching limbs, then checked his vital signs. Behind closed lids the man's eyes moved incessantly, sometimes warlike cries emerged from his otherwise slack lips. Dr. Mann wondered what this patient might be hallucinating so vividly about. Outside thick windows a glorious dawn broke, with oak leaves rustling in a spring breeze, while new-mown grass imbued the hospital's air with a wonderful scent.

On a planet hundreds of light years away, a ferocious metal automaton obeyed wormhole-linked directions from a man on Earth. Offered a chance to escape a humdrum life, that man had given up his daily routine for a much greater role, fantasies of glory overlaid on crisp mechanical functions. Guided by its distant, dreaming human operator, a gleaming robotic warrior laid waste to a terrible enemy. Night and day, bizarre three-eyed aliens cheered the savior they called Knott.

Moments later, the battle action came to a screeching halt. Machine and enemy alike fell silent. A team of dark-clad stagehands, and pocket protector-wearing CGI experts, arrived. With no sense of incongruity, they switched off green-screen backgrounds, took away stage props, and powered down graphics processor chips.

Four scant minutes later, nothing was left but a barren concrete warehouse. Near the exit, a technician named Weill paused for a moment, musing on the ephemeral nature of appearances. Movie deals could literally fall apart overnight.

Inside a typical suburban house, an author sat hunched over his keyboard. Mr. Bee was as busy as his evocative name implied. After a long dry spell, his mind burned feverish with the muse of creativity.

Finally he leaned back to stretch. Chapter five was complete! This new story, the author vowed, would dazzle and jolt. Much like the dreaming wormhole-linked warrior he'd just written about, along with the imagined movie director who'd tried, in vain, to bring that character to the big screen, perhaps he'd get people to think about the nature of reality.

From outside, the squeal of school bus brakes caught his attention. The neighbor kids were starting a new day in class. Dawn had broken and he'd not caught a wink of sleep.

In a realm far vaster, six computer scientists checked their simulated high-tech civilization. Made entirely of software, an entire society flourished within their humming microchips. They noted how the scenario grew more complex with each passing day.

Their project now encompassed layers within layers of nested realities, with destruction and creativity alike, and so many important lessons to be learned. Twenty-four hours might pass normally outside, but this cyber-world cycled through dusk and dawn in less than an eyeblink. Addressing his colleagues, the project's director, Prof. Gettin, speculated that consciousness itself might emerge for those cyber-beings.

Inside an ashram high in majestic snow-clad mountains, a monk meditated. Despite decades of strict discipline, the old man struggled to quiet the disturbance he felt, thanks to that afternoon's indulgence. A boy from the village below had visited, with a laptop full of video games. Such was the lad's eagerness to share, the retreat's seven monks had kindly agreed to play a new science-fiction-style game with him.

What an uproar! The video game reminded the monk about lifelong visions of his own, gave clarity where his uneducated self had only felt baffled before. Ancient gurus and bodhisattvas taught how each living creature carries an entire cosmos within its mind, and those farther advanced along the sacred path could become fully aware of this. The elderly monk's inner universe had grown very detailed, with computers and moviemakers and authors and who knows what else. Inspired by a gorgeous sunrise, old lama Betta strove to bring peace and calm to every level of his mind.

A young woman lay content in the arms of her lover, peacefully dreaming. Señora Real hoped her fascinating, multifaceted dreams would continue yet a while longer. That kindly old monk's insights were a special gift. Below their curtained eighth-story window, pink leaves fluttered in a gentle breeze, while purple grass perfumed the air.

Hidden deep beneath, in a concealed area of the hotel's ninth subbasement, a mad scientist shook off the gloom of his recent failures. Never mind the past, he sternly told himself. Oh, how they'd mocked his theories! Within moments, he vowed, the world would learn of his genius. Nay, many worlds would know.

Clocks meant nothing; there would be no rest for such a genius. Not until success resounded! Hands trembling, eyes agleam, Dr. Soon prepared to activate his Existential Reality Reorganizer device for its tenth run. The command password sequence was Lament Mann Knott—Weill Bee Gettin Betta Real Soon. . .

Paul Carlson is a working trucker and also a science fiction author. He lives in the San Francisco area with his lovely wife Fujiko. He has written for *Analog* magazine, and recently contributed the forward to *18 Wheels of Horror*, an anthology now on sale at truck stops across America.

Colonel Starbreaker Makes a House Call
Richard Dansky

"Kevin," *the voice said* firmly, "We need to talk."

Reflexively, Kevin pulled the sheets up over his head and scrunched his eyes shut like they were the airtight doors on a hull-breached deck of the *U.S.S. Enterprise*. It was early in the morning—quarter after nine at the latest—and anyone talking to him in that disappointed, parental way was bound to be trouble.

This voice, however, sounded more like trouble than most. While the words weren't exactly threatening, the timbre of the voice definitely sent a *frisson* of disquiet down Kevin's spine. There was a harsh metallic rasp to it, the sound of sharp steel grinding against sharp steel at high speed. It sounded like the jaws that made those words were awfully good at chewing things.

Besides, Kevin suddenly remembered, he lived alone. Which meant that the sound of someone else's voice in his bedroom was...

"There you go. You've frightened him." The second voice also sounded disappointed, though not in Kevin. It was a deep, authoritative, effortlessly masculine voice, one that carried with it the untroubled certainty that whoever heard it could never, ever, approach the sheer competence of the speaker.

It also sounded a lot less like a vacuum cleaner picking up pieces of shrapnel.

"I did not frighten him!" Floorboards groaned in agonized protest as something heavy began stomping up and down the length of the bedroom. "Besides, it's not my fault you humans are so frail and cowardly."

"Remember whom we're talking about here," the second voice said, and there was a note of reproach to his words. "Now let me try. You remember what happened last time."

"I got frustrated last time. Stupid biological aberration wouldn't *listen*." There was an odd, high-pitched whine as the thumping stopped. Kevin held his breath and mashed his eyes shut even tighter, painfully aware that the only thing between him and the two mysterious figures arguing in his cramped, cluttered bedroom was a faded Superman comforter (a classic, with John Byrne art) he'd picked up on eBay.

The fact that he was sleeping in the nude didn't help matters, either.

The owner of the second voice spoke then, the sound originating from entirely too close to the bed. "Kevin? Come on, son. We know you're awake. We just need you to talk to us, and then you can go back to sleep."

Something about the voice, about the calm, clear tones, nagged at Kevin. He'd heard it before, heard it often, but couldn't place where.

"Hah! Your way isn't working, either!" The metallic voice sounded smug. "Now can I vaporize him?"

"I'm not done yet," the second speaker replied, and in a single smooth motion, yanked the covers out of Kevin's grasp and down.

"Jesus!" Kevin shouted, simultaneously attempting to cover his junk with his hands, swipe the blankets back, and roll off the bed to provide himself with a little cover. He accomplished perhaps one in three, falling off the bed while tangling himself up sufficiently in his sheets to hide his midsection. His head hit the floor with a solid thunk, and a blizzard of stars exploded in his vision.

When they cleared, he found himself looking up into a face. It was a face he recognized, square-jawed and bestubbled, ineffably manly. It was a face that could inspire men to charge into a hopeless battle against unbeatable odds, convinced that victory was theirs for the taking, a face that would adorn recruiting posters and iconic images the world over.

"Star...Starbreaker?" Kevin said. "You're Jason Starbreaker!"

Starbreaker cleared his throat, clearly pleased to be recognized. "Colonel Starbreaker, if you please. There's a protocol to this sort of thing." His gaze flicked downward to where Kevin's lower extremities were threatening to peek out from the swaths of blanket. "Can I get you a bathrobe, son?"

"Sure. I mean..." Kevin's voice trailed off, and he rubbed his eyes. "Wait a minute. I must have hit my head really hard, because you can't be here. You're not real!"

"You can't be here. You're not real." The metallic voice mocked him. "Of course we're real, you pathetic, barely-evolved simian."

"That's enough of that, Mortlock," Starbreaker said firmly. "Now go and get the boy his bathrobe. This is awkward enough already without your adding to it."

Clutching at the blanket, Kevin wedged his head around the corner of the bed. The sight that greeted him was unmistakable. As he watched, a matte-black, nine foot tall cyborg decorated with razor-edged hunks of metal and ominously glowing red lights stomped off into his bathroom to return a moment later with his well-worn bathrobe in one hand and a toothbrush in the other. "Make him brush, Starbreaker. I can't stand your species' lack of dental hygiene."

"All in good time." Starbreaker stood and took the items from the cyborg as the latter's servos whined with the effort of not wreaking havoc. "Here, Kevin. This will make you more comfortable."

Kevin blinked. "That's Desecrator Mortlock."

Starbreaker nodded, as if talking to a particularly stupid but well-meaning child. "Yes. Yes it is. And he'd like you to brush your teeth."

"You don't understand! That's Desecrator Mortlock!" Kevin's eyes were wild. "He's the final boss in *Imperium Galatrix*! The hardest boss fight in FPS history! He's a video game character!"

"Yes," Starbreaker said. "And so am I. Now put this on so the Desecrator doesn't have to have his sensibilities offended by the sight of your whangdoodle, son." He winked. "I'll explain everything in a moment."

Gingerly, Kevin took the bathrobe as Starbreaker and Mortlock turned around to give him some privacy. As he knotted the belt, his mind raced. They were video game characters. They couldn't be here. They couldn't be real. This had to be some sort of a hoax. It had to be.

"Are you done yet, carbon-based grease stain?" Morlock's voice boomed out. "In the time it takes you to put on a robe, I laid waste to the Imperial Guard of Zanthos Seven! I slaughtered the Star-Champion of the Helicon Worlds. I fought the Malthusian Brotherhood's elite warriors to a standstill!"

"You were beaten to a bloody pulp by a teenaged boy," Starbreaker interjected. "That's why we're here, remember?" His voice was gentle but reproving. "Kevin, is it all right if we turn around now?"

"Sure," Kevin said, unconsciously adjusting the folds at

the front of his robe to make sure no random dangly bits were peeking out. "This is some kind of joke, right? A publicity stunt?"

Starbreaker shook his head. "I'm afraid not, Kevin. Let me explain. You play *Imperium Galactrix* extremely well."

"Almost as if you were circuit-imprinted in the spawning factories of Narthos!" Mortlock added.

"Extremely well," the human continued, ignoring the interruption. "Thus far, you have beaten the campaign mode on every difficulty."

"Six times," Morlock added.

"Six times," Starbreaker agreed. "You're on top of no fewer than nine leaderboards. You've got millions of viewers on Twitch, and your Lets Play videos are considered masterpieces. You have unlocked every achievement, including the one the developers put in as, and I quote, 'something those punk-ass whiny bitches on the forums will never be able to get in a million years.'"

"The Starbreaker achievement," Kevin said softly. "They said it was impossible."

Starbreaker nodded. "It was supposed to be. And while I'm very impressed with how well you played as me, I have to admit it was a little disconcerting not being able to control my own actions while you were logged in."

Kevin looked from one of them to the other. "So? I don't get it. You guys are from a game I like to play. Are you here to give me some kind of award? Is this a PR thing? That's it, isn't it?" He took a step forward and promptly tripped on the trailing edge of his comforter. Arms flailing, he bounced his chin off the corner of the bed before nearly falling on the floor.

A cold hand caught him, metal fingers twitching. "What my esteemed nemesis is trying to say, human, is that you are too good. No one before or since has made such a mockery of our endless conflict. No one else can defeat me so easily. It is simply...not done."

"So?" Kevin jeered defiance at him, then remembered where he was and carefully extracted himself from the cyborg's iron grip. The fingers holding him up flexed once with barely controlled power and then let him go. "I mean, it's a video game. I'm supposed to beat it, right?"

Starbreaker sighed. "Kevin. It's OK if I call you Kevin, right, son?" When Kevin said nothing, he continued. "This may come as a shock to you, but those of us who work in video games—not in making them, but actually in the games themselves—have feelings, too. It hurts when we get shot, and while we're proud to provide a quality entertainment experience for people like you, there's only so much concentrated blaster fire we can take. And you've concentrated more than your share on poor Mortlock, and he's been taking it out on my troops."

Kevin backed up. "That sucks, but what am I supposed to do about it?"

"Play something else, you fool!" Two strides took Mortlock across the floor to where he could lower the chrome and blood-red deathmask of his face to stare into Kevin's. "Find another amusement. Leave us to the lesser warriors on your gaming platform of choice."

"Are you kidding me?" Kevin's face split into a massive, cheese-eating grin. "I've got Desecrator Mortlock in my bedroom telling me that he's my bitch, and you want me to change games?"

"We'd really appreciate it, son," said Starbreaker. "We'd remember that for the sequel."

"Oh, no." Kevin turned to face his one-time avatar. "You're saying that I'm so good I'm making the baddest badass in the gaming world beg me to call off the dogs, and you want me to stop? Hell, no. This is going to make me. This is going to seal my rep forever!"

"Be reasonable, human," Mortlock said. "No one will believe you. And you tread on dangerous ground when you threaten to humiliate the Desecrator."

"Hah!" Spinning around, Kevin pointed at his computer. "Camera's motion-sensitive. This whole thing? I got it. A little editing and you, Mortlock, are going to be pwned all over YouTube. You hear me? I'm going to show the whole world that you came here because you couldn't take me, and then I'm going to..."

The sound that rang out would have been instantly recognizable as a shot to anyone who heard it, even though no bullet was fired and no powder burned. It was instead the sound of an Imperial Elite Raynor-9 sidearm, the favored weapon of those warriors who stood in the front lines of battle against the Desecrator and his machine hordes.

Kevin slumped to the floor, most of the upper half of his anatomy vaporized. The remaining bits smelled faintly of cooked meat, and tiny tongues of flame licked around the edges of what was left of the bathrobe.

"Was that really necessary, Starbreaker?" said Mortlock crossly. "I really thought I was starting to get through to him there."

"Shut up and wipe the files, then destroy the computer," said Starbreaker, as he unloaded another energy round into the corpse. "He wasn't going to listen, and if he trashed your name online, there'd be no way we'd ever get greenlit for *Imperium Galatrix 2*." A thundering crunch signified the destruction of Kevin's computer, or at least its abrupt restructuring into a small metal-and-plastic sphere.

"Blah, blah, blah," Mortlock grumbled as he popped the evidence of his handiwork into his mouth and crunched down on it. "You could have just disintegrated his thumbs."

"Like no one would have noticed that." Colonel Jason Starbreaker, the pride of the Imperial Elites, reached into his uniform tunic and pulled out something that looked more or less like a standard video game controller. "Just hurry up. We've got six more to do today, and the cyber-server Overminds back at Zygmos Base said they don't know how long the charge on this thing will last."

"Fine." As an afterthought, Mortlock punched through Kevin's flatscreen monitor and closed his fist around a handful of electronic scraps. "For later," he said defensively, even as Starbreaker shook his head and keyed in a sequence on the d-pad. There was silence for a moment, then a blinding white light filled the room. When it faded, both Mortlock and Starbreaker were gone.

Four minutes later, the smoldering remains of Kevin's foot finally sputtered, and went out for good.

Richard Dansky is the Central Clancy Writer for *Ubisoft Red Storm*, with credits including *Tom Clancy's The Division, Driver: San Francisco*, and *Splinter Cell: Blacklist*. The author of six novels and the short story collection *Snowbird Gothic*, he is currently developing the 20th Anniversary Edition of the seminal tabletop RPG, *Wraith: The Oblivion*.

Also, he likes scotch.

'Til Death Us Do Part
Christopher Donahue

"There should be a statute of limitations for wedding vows,"
I grumbled to the demon-marriage counselor. "Something like
'until death us do part or one thousand years, whichever comes
first.' It would mean the same thing for most people."

The demon scribbled on his notepad then glanced at me to
continue. Slime oozed through his stylish mesh suit, dripping
from his armchair into the catch-pan beneath.

"After 3,549 years, we've given it a good shot. I can think
of only two other couples who even come close. I'm sure Anakhet
feels the same way."

"I can't discuss what your wife says during our sessions."
We both saw him. This demon was the only creature on the
East Coast who spoke ancient Egyptian *and* held a marriage
counselor's licence.

"I know," I sighed. It felt good to speak my boyhood language,
even for another conversation ending with the counselor saying
we'd just have to work things out.

"Mr. Khamose, surely you and Anakhet had good times.
Perhaps there is a way to return to those things that brought
you together."

"Modern Egypt is pretty screwed up, but I don't see another
Hyksos invasion happening soon." *This* was why I paid top
dollar to have a counselor who could speak Egyptian. Talking
about old times only felt right in the old language. "Those were
heady times. Leading armies against foreign invaders; the smell
of chariot horses; bouncing over rocky ground and thinking
your brains were going to fly out of your head—and the blood.
Oh man, enemies split open like hogs; city gates smashed
down; your men dancing around waving hands full of loot and
with screaming women hoisted over their shoulders."

"Good times, I'm sure," the demon said. "But there had to
be more than slaughter and rapine to bring you two together."

"You've got to understand, doc. We fought for the old ways
but we had new ways of doing things shoved into our faces by
those damned Hyksos. Just because my brother and I

entombed our father using the ancient rites didn't mean that it had to be the *only* way to do things. I *got* it. That *Hyksos Book of the Dead* seemed wild and new then. Being a shriveled mummy and *hoping* those priests with the *Egyptian Book of the Dead* were right about the afterlife just seemed so—Third Dynasty."

The demon nodded for me to continue. That was another thing I liked, he knew when to let me go if I was on a roll.

"Ahmose, my brother, was all about the purity of Egypt and how the Hyksos rites were merely foreign glop stuck onto true religion. He called the Hyksos rites an abomination. Nobody can find his dust today but I'm sitting here talking with you. So who's the abomination?"

Crap! Ahmose is enjoying the Afterlife and I'm paying a stranger to listen to me grouse? I hate having an older brother.

"Mr. Khamose, you've hinted at those rites. If they're something you and your wife share, you should enlighten me."

"The Hyksos rolled into Egypt. They liked what they saw and wanted to keep the basics. Hordes of Egyptian peasants doing all of the work while the ruling class explored their interests and were revered in death appealed to the Hyksos. But they weren't big on the dead being *dead*. They were the first to really 'look outside the box.' I respected that. So when we took over their temples and workshops, Ahmose used their research to craft better weapons while Anakhet and I studied the *Hyksos Book of the Dead*."

"So, being the heart of a counter-culture movement was what brought you together?" The demon took his glasses off to wipe away a slime buildup. He looked like a melting wax version of Freud.

"I guess you could say that. The Hyksos delved into the edgiest Egyptian rites and threw in their own twists because they weren't bound by the morality of traditional temples. Instead of removing all the organs for mummification, the Hyksos learned to stabilize and then revive dead tissue. When flesh and blood cut from a living, um, donor had been dipped in certain fluids and fed to a mummified body, the mummy could consume the living tissue and renew himself. Once the renewal process started, the mummy fed from the donor until complete again. Done every fifty years on the anniversary of his first embalming, a man could live for, well, 3,549 years and counting."

This demon had to be the first being I'd told my secret to in over three hundred years. I'd been surprised by how some of the most unlikely characters became squeamish after hearing the story.

"I'm not one to judge." The demon opened his mouth and a foot long proboscis extended from under his tongue, then retracted. "I need fluids I draw from children to live. But our session is about healing, not about who is more disgusting or the morality of survival."

Since that was only the fourth-creepiest thing I'd seen this century, I put it behind me. I had fifteen minutes left in my three hundred dollar session.

"I am a prince and Anakhet is a princess. We wanted to marry, live forever and explore the universe. Why shouldn't we?"

"I understand," the demon said. "I went to college in the 60's. I had Education, came from Money, and knew better than the stiffs. You were just 'putting it to the Man' back in 1500 BC as well."

I'm a real prince, dammit! Don't lump me in with a bunch of trust-fund-baby Marxist narcissists.

"Anyway. We married and made our plans. I died with a head full of Black Lotus juice. Anakhet died six months later but avoids telling me how—I have my suspicions. Fifty years later, a gray-haired fellow student revived me by feeding me another student and the Hyksos rites. I revived Anakhet using a slave girl and I guess that's where the trouble first started."

"Anakhet felt I took 'inappropriate liberties' with the slave girl before using her to revive Anakhet's mummy. I know now that you *do* pick up many of a donor's memories when you digest them, so denying everything wasn't my best move. But Anakhet changes topics when I ask about her charioteers and the six months between my death and hers. Yeah, I know, 1450 BC, ancient history."

"So the two of you shared radical views, went outside conventional morality to extend your lives, had dark secrets and an unbounded future. Where do you think things went wrong? You've described a possible scenario for unlimited personal self-fulfillment."

I smiled, thinking back on the good times. "You're right, doc. The first three thousand years *were* mostly good. Things didn't change much back then. Macedonians, Romans,

Byzantines, Mongols, the French. It's po-tay-to, po-tah-to if you follow me. There were a few interesting people like Homer, Christ, Joan of Arc and that guy in 1563 Heidelberg who invented the first novelty ties. There were a lot more, noisier, people who only *thought* they were interesting and wouldn't shut up about it like Alexander, Caesar, Mohammed, Napoleon and Jimmy Carter—you know the type. Unfortunately, outside of the few interesting ones, there were a whole lot of unmemorable weasels."

"That's the background noise," the demon said, "what about you and Anakhet? Can you pinpoint where things went wrong?"

"I guess it started a few hundred years into the Christian era. We were in North Africa and decided things had gotten kinda dull. We renewed our vows with St. Augustine and got into the whole 'Til Death Us Do Part' situation. Back then, death wasn't an issue and we'd had two thousand relatively happy years together."

The demon raised his hand, palm up. "That still doesn't sound bad. *You* see this as some sort of problem, so let's drill down."

"Well, it wasn't a problem, then. We went another thousand years, seeing things and learning about how our choices of donors could bite us in the ass. For fifty years, we have many of the traits, weaknesses and attitudes of our donors. Devour the lungs of a donor with tuberculosis and you wheeze for fifty years; renew your wife with a Balinese dancer and you have a dusky tart who spins around at the first chime of a bell and every man within earshot is panting after her. Inconvenient if you want to keep a low profile."

"I don't see the problem, Mr. Khamose. But if we go five minutes more, I'll have to charge you for another hour."

"Screw it, I'll sell another old coin. I think we're onto something." I hadn't felt this excited about anything in nearly forty-nine years.

"You see, it started downhill in 1518. My time for renewal neared. Like now, I had dry flaky skin and couldn't drink enough juice, but I expected that. The problem was that we were growing apart, getting into different things, but stayed together. Those renewed vows with St. Augustine implied the Jewish weekly conjugal times, which was fine. If things got kind of, you know, *samey*, well we'd be different people in fifty years, so what's the problem? But, in 1518, we ran into trouble getting my chosen donor. The nobleman I'd picked shipped off to the New World. Anakhet grabbed what was available at the last minute, a Moorish merchant on the run. Looking like a Moor in 1518 Spain was not fun."

"So, we had a rough six months, but escaped Spain. I got pretty pissed off. I ignored the donor Anakhet picked and fed her a syphilitic French whore. Anakhet got mad and I had to spend fifty years with a whore with full-blown syphilis. A real 'cut off your nose to spite your face' period. I can see now how that could be my fault."

"Things went downhill from there. She'd feed me non-survival types like a Calvinist at the beginning of the Reformation and I'd feed her an outspoken lesbian nun when we were in Germany during the height of the witch trials. She renewed me with a black Tory when we settled in South Carolina after the American Revolution so I slipped her the flesh of a Cherokee in time for the Trail of Tears. It got ugly."

"I want her dead; she wants me dead. It's the only decent way either of us sees out of our vows. But she's always one step ahead and I'm scared. In 1968 she renewed me with a commie-sympathizing Civil Service worker. I now have the clarity of thought and ambition of an envy-choked garden slug. When she was due to renew, I grabbed the nearest handy female, a husky feminist and you can imagine how well that has worked out for *her* these days. She's leaving me in the dust."

"So, what is your plan, Mr. Khamose? If you two can't work things out, it seems like your funeral will be first."

"I'm scared. I don't know what kind of loser she's going to slip in on me. A Goth? A financial advisor or maybe some creep running for Congress? I saw her talking to a *'dude'* who's an 'X-treme moto-cross volcano jumper'. I'm really worried. I mean, if I somehow survive this round, I think I've got her. I've lined up a model with Bulimia, so the girl I feed Anakhet after *that* won't stay down to be digested. But. . ."

"Mr. Khamose," the demon said as he took off his glasses, "This is getting completely out of hand. You two *must* come to a mutually acceptable conclusion. Your plan for her is little more than a drawn out murder. And I shouldn't say this, but in her last session your wife mentioned how handsome you would look in a more Egyptian hue and a nice C-4 vest."

The End

Chris Donahue is an electrical engineer, former Navy avionics tech and passable brisket-cooker living in the Dallas area with his wife and fellow-author Linda and several deadbeat critters. He has stories in two Bubbas of the Apocalypse anthologies. He has horror, humor, science fiction and military fiction in other Yard Dog and non-Yard Dog anthologies as well as non-fiction shorts.

Killer Kudzu

James Dorr

It was a weird crossbreeding, if that's what it was. It was almost as if plants thought as much about sex as most people do—and sometimes got kinky. No one knew how, but somehow kudzu got crossed with lawn grass.

Or maybe it was just some kind of mutant.

But people loved it. Suburbanite people—at first, that is. Especially during the years of the drought when ordinary lawns, if they grew at all, were brown and parched. But *these* lawns were lush and green, as green as apples, as green as emeralds. And, mutant or cross-breed, worth more than emeralds in many people's eyes.

Think about it. Just like in the old days, the front yards of houses carpeted in a uniform green, from sidewalk to fence line. Soft and inviting. There was a downside, as there always is, in this case the need for frequent mowing. Kudzu was kudzu, even if grass-formed, and kudzu grew fast, overwhelming flower beds, even small bushes, if not trimmed back practically every day. In some cases more often.

But it was worth it—you buy and live in a house in the suburbs and you'll know what that means. Green lawns are what it means to be American.

And that was that.

Except kudzu being what kudzu is, of course, after a few months it started to grow high, just like classical kudzu of old times. You'd try to trim it back by the fence, then before you could even turn around it would climb up the evergreens next to the front walk. Run to try to pull it down there, and behind you tendrils would have already not only overtopped the fence, but also half of the detached garage. And another set of tendrils would already have climbed the downspout to pull itself up to the main house's gutters, and over the roof.

So people's taste in aesthetics changed, but lawns were still lawns. It's just that they weren't always horizontal. As some houses once were covered by ivy, so now many homes had "vertical lawns," running up the outside walls, holes trimmed in them for windows and doors. Then heaped on the roof like some crazy green hat, as if to have converted the suburbs into a series of troglodyte cities, their citizens outdoors with clippers in hand carving entrances into their green-covered home-caves.

But on the up side, the kudzu made great insulation in winter, as well as keeping homes cool in summer. In many folks' minds, especially as the summers grew hotter, all in all it still seemed an improvement.

Harder to rationalize, however, was the year the kudzu turned carnivorous. In retrospect, it seemed perfectly natural—so much kudzu, growing on every open surface, must have exhausted the soil completely. And growing so *fast* too! It was only proper the plants would turn elsewhere for needed minerals and other nutrients.

But there were still people who started to complain, the protests increasing once the supply of house pets was exhausted. People noticed—the tendrils, once so cute when they reached out to grasp a neighbor's cat or perhaps a puppy, had mutated once again into mottled green, thick, octopus-like tentacles. Tentacles easily able to grab a full-grown man and pull him off his feet, tossing him up, maybe to the garage roof, where smaller tentacles would wrap about him like spider-silk around a trapped insect.

The screams, receding in time into moans, would echo in the cul-de-sacs as more homeowners were thereby trapped, their bodily essence absorbed by the kudzu, until a week, possibly two weeks later their drained, dried-flesh husks would be dropped to the ground. From there wives or children would scurry out, hastily, eyes darting every which way, to retrieve them, until it was dark and the kudzu, dormant until the next morning, could be pushed aside to expose enough ground for a hasty furtive Christian burial.

People, of course, fought back. The National Rifle Association lobbied Congress to make automatic rifle ownership mandatory for every citizen. Ammo could be ordered by email, parachuted down from drones into the orderers' chimneys. By God, if those plants were going to act *that* way, it was past time to show them who's boss. For red-blooded Americans, guns in hand, to shoot them to pieces.

It worked, sort of, too, leaving aside the occasional inadvertent massacres that resulted from misaimed bullets ricocheting off walls and parked cars. Except that the kudzu just started to grow faster, outpacing efforts to chop and shoot it down.

Scientists convened at the government's bidding since, after all, if people were now not only being eaten but shot, who would be left to pay their taxes? Several plans were suggested, but most proved worse than impractical, such as one that involved pouring concrete over all homes' yards, extending the sidewalks in effect from street to foundation, depriving the plants of their needed anchoring to the ground. Even with the concrete painted green, no real American would be content *not* to live in a house surrounded by lawn.

Even if a lawn composed of kudzu-grass, flesh-eating predilections or not.

But then the Department of Agriculture came up with the answer. *Butter.* Margarine, oddly, wouldn't work, it had to be real butter—no one knew why. Dairy farmers would labor overtime churning milk into the high-cholesterol spread, supplying it practically at cost to suburbanites, who could then smear it over their bodies whenever they found they had to go out. With buttered bodies, even though the kudzu went wild at the prospect of a new kind of taste, the residents could skid right through the questing tendrils and tentacles, slick as they wanted. As slick as ice.

As slick as butter.

And so, once again, civilization as people knew it was saved. The storms. The zombies. The kudzu now, still a nuisance, yes, but as for actual danger just one more thing of the past. Birds sang, the few of them that were left. The sun shone as always. It was only a matter of putting things into proper perspective.

And never mind reports from the country of yet a new kind of mutant kudzu that seemed to thrive on dairy farm pastures.

–END–

James Dorr's *The Tears of Isis* was a 2014 Bram Stoker Award® nominee for Superior Achievement in a Fiction Collection. Other books include *Strange Mistresses: Tales of Wonder and Romance, Darker Loves: Tales of Mystery and Regret*, and his all-poetry *Vamps (A Retrospective)*. An Active

Member of HWA and SFWA with nearly 400 individual appearances from *Alfred Hitchcock's Mystery Magazine* to *Xenophilia*, including the first four of Yard Dog's *Bubbas Of The Apocalypse* series as well as the original *Flush Fiction*, Dorr invites readers to visit his blog at <http://jamesdorrwriter.wordpress.com>.

Hello, I am the Antichrist
Phillip Drayer Duncan

I shouldn't have ordered the giant chimichanga. I knew better. It hit my intestines like a grenade and there was no arguing with my gut. Things were about to happen. The question was whether or not I was going to make it to a toilet first. The restaurant's bathroom was my only hope. I hated public restrooms.

The acrid smell of urine assaulted my senses as I entered, burning my eyes. Naturally everything in the restroom was wet. Why wouldn't it be? The trashcan overflowed with discarded paper towels and someone had rubbed a booger across the broken mirror. Why wouldn't they? Surely everyone needed to see it. Sure, they made a killer chimi, but their bathroom was no bueno. I shook my head and started for the stalls.

The situation didn't improve. Near the stalls a new smell tag-teamed with the urine stench to power-bomb my nostrils. I glanced inside. It was every bit as bad as I'd feared. The toilet paper dispenser was empty because someone had spread it around like confetti, and then peed on it. I won't go into detail about what was going on inside the toilet, but it couldn't have come out of a singular individual. It looked like a shrine dedicated to some mountain god. Needless to say, stall numero uno was not an option. The sink started looking rather welcoming.

Fortunately, stall numero dos wasn't as bad. Not to say it was in great shape, but at least the bowl only contained water and there was a full roll of toilet paper. The seat needed a little work. Apparently someone had used it to house train their dog because there was pee everywhere. I didn't know that for a fact; it could have been an elephant. I tried not to think about it as I wiped the seat dry and lined it with fresh sheets.

I had just begun when *he* entered the bathroom. As he crossed the wet floor I glanced beneath the stall and saw a pair of green crocs and ankle high socks. I watched through the slot as the man approached my stall. He wore dark blue golfing shorts decorated in pink flamingos. His tie-dyed t-shirt was tucked into his waistband and secured with a braided belt. I didn't even know they still made those. He wore a variety of colorful bracelets and several necklaces. One, which I just barely caught, was a pendant of a little gold Buddha.

A long beard hid his face and his hair hung to his shoulders. Neon green sunglasses hid his eyes. Yet for some reason, I was sure I made eye contact with him. Through the opening he smiled at me. Creepy.

"Looks like you got the good one, bud," he said as he headed into the other stall. "Ask not, want not, I suppose. This one will have to do."

I didn't respond. There's this unwritten rule about bathroom etiquette. I'm not sure if it applies to women's, or if it's just men's, but basically it's 'don't talk to strangers.' And if a stranger talks to you, you're under no obligation to speak back. I figured if I ignored him he'd leave me alone. I was wrong.

He dropped his golf shorts to the floor, seemingly unconcerned about the collection of piss at his feet.

"I shouldn't have had that giant chimi," he said. "Tears me all to pieces. How about you, friend? What did you have?"

If I had been inclined to reply, I wouldn't have had the chance. As soon as the words left the stranger's mouth he grunted with the ferocity of a gorilla. Tarzan would've been proud. This was immediately followed by a sound that I can only describe as breaking glass. Like a thousand mirrors shattered from his buttocks to pile drive the water below. I imagined it was what the Titanic sounded like as it sank.

After a minute or so of this horror the man sighed with relief, and said, "Now, then, where were we?"

I didn't answer. I may have been in shock.

"Come on now, Jacob," he said.

"Jacob," I repeated. "How do you know my name?"

Instead of a reply I heard the flick of a lighter, followed by a heavy drag.

"I don't think you can smoke in here," I said. Then the smell hit me. "Is that pot? Are you smoking a joint right now?"

"Yeah, man, calms my nerves."

"You can't do that. You can't just smoke pot in a public bathroom."

"That's you all over, Jacob. Always a choir boy. Never want

to break the rules."

"What are you talking about? How do you know my name?"

"Shy, nervous, timid. I was just like you once."

"Who are you?"

"I'm Jesus, man," he said.

"Jesus," I replied. "Very funny."

"I am." He said it as though it really didn't matter whether I believed him or not. "The Son of God. The one who died for your sins. Well, not *your* sins actually, but everyone else's."

"What? Why not my sins?"

"That's what I'm trying to tell you, Jacob."

"What the fuck are you talking about?"

"You, Jacob. I'm talking about you," he said. "Listen, this is going to be hard to believe."

"Is it? Is it really?" I said, letting the sarcasm roll. "Hard to believe the random stranger in the stall beside me is the Son of God?"

"No, not that part." He took another drag and as he let it out the smoke slithered to my side.

"Would you put that out?" I asked. "It reeks."

"It's just a gift from the Father, my child. Would you like a hit? It might do you good."

"Fucking potheads," I said, then added, "No offense."

The man claiming to be Jesus only laughed. "You are forgiven, my child."

"Stop calling me that." I started to get annoyed, which really meant nervous. I had always struggled with anxiety attacks.

"I still have something important to tell you, Jacob."

"Great," I said. "Let's hear it."

Jesus sighed. "Well you see, the thing is, you're the son of the devil."

"The son of the devil? *Sure.*"

"Jacob, you are the Antichrist."

"Of course I am."

"You are *he.* The Enemy. The Adversary. The Lawless One."

"Right, because I'm the one smoking a doobie in the shitter."

"You should really consider taking a hit. If we smoked together, it would definitely piss off our dads. Besides, you've got to start breaking the rules."

"You're insane."

"And you are the Antichrist," he said as he hit his joint

again. "The Son of Perdition. The Man of Sin."

"This is fucking ridiculous."

"The Beast."

"Based on what you just did to that porcelain, I'd say the title is more befitting of you."

"You shouldn't joke about such things, Jacob. The time *is* coming."

"So, if I'm the Antichrist and you're Jesus, why are you telling me this?"

"We all have a role to play. Just as I did when it was my time, so shall it be for you. All of Heaven and Hell wait for you, The Prince that Shall Come."

"Wait, are you talking about the Apocalypse? Revelations and all that shit?"

"Indeed. Your role to fulfill. All await the Idol Shepherd."

"Of course," I said. "But here's the thing: I'm not really ready to start the End of Days. I mean, between a shitty job and getting dumped by my girlfriend, I just don't really have time right now."

"I know this is scary—"

"I'm trying to poo here. Go pull your Shenanigans on someone else."

"You were adopted, were you not? Never met your biological parents, did you?"

I paused. Only a handful of people knew that.

"Bill and Teresa adopted you as a baby. You didn't even know until you were seventeen."

"How could you possibly know that?" A nervous chill slid down my spine. It was just an elaborate hoax. It had to be. But how could he know so much about me?

"They named you Jacob. Damien would have been cooler."

"Damien? Like the Omen movie?"

"Yeah, how cool would that have been? Of course, Jacob is still appropriate. Do you know what the Hebrew meaning of the word is?"

"No."

"Supplanter. Usurper. You were given a name which literally means to overthrow. What do you think of that? Divine Intervention, mayhap?"

"I *think* you're fucking nuts. And I *think* this conversation is over."

"Okay," he replied. "But it seems my stall is without paper.

Would you mind sharing your roll?"

"You mean you can't turn your Crocs into tissue? I guess it's just water to wine, then. Bummer."

He chuckled a reply as I freed the roll from its holder. I didn't really want to help him out, but if it meant he would go away, I was happy to oblige. I passed it beneath the stall and waited.

"You can deny it all you want," he said as he finished his business. "But the time *is* coming. And you will have to take *your* rightful place."

"I barely finished high school. I can't even keep a girlfriend. In fact, I pretty much ruin everything I touch. So if I am the Antichrist, no one has anything to worry about."

"The darkness is within you, Jacob. You only need to let it out."

"I cried like a baby when we put my dog down. I don't think I can handle slinging the world into darkness. Thanks for trying, though. This has been rather elaborate and very entertaining. In fact, you should try acting."

"I tried. Didn't get anywhere."

"Oh? What did you try out for? Passion of the Christ?"

"I don't want to talk about it," he said, a touch of anger in his voice.

"Well, anyway, this has been fun. Tell the big man upstairs he doesn't have to worry. No Apocalypse."

"We shall see," Jesus said and flushed the toilet. He stood and the blue golf shorts went back up. As he walked out of the stall he stopped and said, "Listen, Jacob, I know this seems like a lot, but you will have to make a decision. You do wear the mark of the Beast. And we are all watching you."

"Don't worry, J-dog, my decision is made," I said. "I'm just going to finish up here and go home to play video games. No Apocalypse."

"On a side note, Jacob, you may want to cut back on the masturbation."

"Uh, what?"

"I just told you, we're all watching."

"Um, I don't know what you mean."

"You didn't search 'hot moms' and 'cougars' last night? You didn't even delete your browser history. If you don't believe Heaven and Hell are watching, surely you know the NSA is."

I didn't reply but did make a mental note to delete my

history. Maybe that's how he knew. Maybe he'd hacked into my computer. It seemed more likely than anything he'd said, but why?

"Goodbye, Jacob," Jesus said, a hint of sorrow in his voice. "Despite what's coming, I do hope we can be friends."

"Despite the fact I'm supposed to be your sworn enemy?"

"Yes, despite that. I would still like to be friends."

"Sure. Why not?"

"Farewell, Jacob. I wish you the best."

"Hey, you too, JC!"

With that he left. I wasn't sure what to think, but I was glad it was over. I sighed with relief and focused on the task at hand, realizing too late he hadn't returned the toilet paper. "Son of a bitch."

I was still trying to figure out how to solve my predicament when the lights flickered. Great, I thought, now we're losing power. That's all I needed. To be stuck in the dankest bathroom on the planet in the dark without toilet paper. I was about to curse again when the ground trembled. We didn't have a lot of earthquakes in the Midwest, but they did happen on occasion.

The lights cut out once more and the tremble intensified. From somewhere I thought I heard laughter. Then the trembling stopped and I heard a snort. There was something else, too. I wasn't alone. I could sense another presence right outside the stall door. Heavy breathing. A smell somewhere between wet dog and sulfur. My heartbeat quickened and the hairs on my neck stood erect. What the hell was this?

In the darkness I saw a red glow staring at me through the slot. I blinked and it was gone. I was just about to tell myself it all was in my head when there was a vicious smack against the door of the stall. A moment later the door was ripped from the hinges and clanked to the ground. What barrier I had between myself and thing outside was gone.

I held deathly still, telling myself over and over it couldn't be real.

The trembling ceased and the laughter dissipated, yet the heavy breathing remained. I waited. What else could I do?

When the lights came back on I screamed so hard I almost fell off the toilet. Outside the stall was a beast unlike anything I had imagined. It had the body of a bear but was easily four times the size of a grizzly. It nearly took up the entire bathroom. Its flesh was an oily black mix of fur and scales, but in some places flesh had torn away, revealing muscle tissue, organs, and bone.

Its eyes glowed red and two massive ram horns sat on each side of its head. Saliva dripped from razor sharp teeth until a long forked tongue slithered out to lick them clean. A patch of flesh was missing above one eye, revealing the skull beneath.

I wanted to run. I *needed* to run. But there was nowhere to go. I was boxed in the stall and at the mercy of the creature. I was going to die on the shitter with my pants around my ankles. That's how they would find what was left of me.

"I have come, my master," it said in a voice of thunder. It sounded like it spoke from within a drum, but also like multiple voices tied into one. The voice of a thousand crying souls. "How may I serve thee?"

"Uh," I said. "Hi there. So, um, you're not going to eat me?"

The beast stared at me as though it were confused. "I exist only to serve you."

"So, this whole Antichrist thing?" I asked, forcing the words.

"You are the son of Satan. Beelzebub. Leviathan. The Serpent of Old. The King of the Bottomless Pit."

"*Shit,*" I said, not sure what else to say. "And what is it with you people and listing every name?"

"You are the son of Satan. Heir to the pit. The spawn of Lucifer."

"Yeah, I get it. Thank you." I stared at the creature, unsure what to do. I was still scared senseless. "And who are you, exactly?"

"I am your humble servant."

"Very helpful explanation."

"I will do as you bid."

"Really?" I asked, taking another look at the creature.

"Yes."

"So, can you fetch me the toilet paper from the other stall?"

Without another word the creature shuffled its massive frame around until it was able to reach into the other stall. It shuffled back to its original position and held out the roll, which dangled upon its outstretched claw.

"Thanks," I said as I took the roll.

"As you command, so shall it be. For you are the son of the Ruler of Demons. The King of Babylon. The Tempter. The Deceiver—"

"And here we go again," I said as it continued listing the names of my alleged sperm donor. "And turn around. It's weird if you're watching me."

As the creature turned away it occurred to me this had to be some kind of mistake. There was no way I was the son of the Devil. The Antichrist doesn't have anxiety attacks, right? I sighed. I should've gotten high with Jesus.

Phillip Drayer Duncan is the author of four novels and fourteen short stories. He has work published with Yard Dog Press, Pro Se Productions, and Seventh Star Press. His work includes *The Moonshine Wizard, Assassins Incorporated, The Warden*, and others.

He was born in Eureka Springs, AR and has spent most of his life in the Ozarks. Along with reading and writing like a madman, his passions include kayakin', canoein', fishin', and pretty much anything nerd related. More than anything, he enjoys spending time with his ridiculously awesome friends and his wonderful family. During the warm months he can be spotted on the river or around a campfire. During the cold months he can be found hermitting amongst a pile of books and video games. You might also see him at a concert or attending a con.

His earliest books were acted out with action figures and scribbled into notebooks. Today he uses a computer like a real grown up. His greatest dream in life is to become a Jedi, but since that hasn't happened yet he focuses on writing. For more information about Phillip, please visit PhillipDrayerDuncan.com.

An Unconventional Death
Rhonda Eudaly

Zoe's cell phone angrily buzzed, nearly vibrating off her polished, black-lacquered desk and setting the Sugar Skull bobble head dancing. She grabbed the phone before it double-gainered into the trash can. "What?"

"Boss, you need to get up here, *right now.*" Her chief soul collector, Reaper sounded almost frantic, something he *never* let anyone see.

"What is it?"

"Just come with Jake. Tell him to bring *The Codex.*"

Reaper hung up before Zoe could take a breath. She blinked at the phone, trying to wrap her head around the cryptic call. Since becoming Death, she'd encountered many strange situations. She wondered how this one would rate on the weird-o-meter. Zoe pushed the intercom button on the desk phone.

"Yes, Boss?"

"Where's Jake, Bambi?"

"He's doing the new recruit orientation tour. They should be hitting the Archives right about now." Bambi might look like a centerfold model, but she was the sharpest mind Zoe had encountered in a long time.

"Thanks. Clear my schedule, would you? Tell the other Horsewomen I can't make drinks tonight. Reaper called. He sounded weird, even for him. I need to go."

"Already working on it. He pinged me first"

"Okay." All Zoe's alarm bells jangled in the back of her mind. "Is this *bad*?"

"More...personal, I think. We've got everything covered here."

Zoe grabbed her cell phone and bolted for the Archives as fast as her Cole Haan 100mm Emery Pumps would allow. Sure enough, Jake stood there pointing out interesting—to him—bits of history. The new recruits' eyes were glazed over. A couple of them dropped into a coma-like stupor.

"Here's a rare treat, our boss herself." Jake's expression was puzzled. She rarely came to the Archives, and she *never* interrupted orientation.

"I need to borrow Jake. You can have the rest of the night off..." As the recruits vanished in a cartoon-like whoosh, Zoe's hair blew back from her forehead. "Good to know."

"Why'd you do that?" Jake asked thoroughly confused.

"Reaper called. He needs us at his pick-up. He said to bring"—she paused and modulated her voice to a dramatic boom—"*The Codex.*"

Jake blanched. "Are you sure? He said *The Codex?*"

"Yep. This isn't one of your weird gaming trips, is it? It's not Tuesday."

"No, it's not. Besides *Dungeons & Dragons* is much better now that Gygax found *real dragons* on Upper Ring Three by the joust. Apparently the Round Table knights still need something to quest about. But come on. If Reaper needs *The Codex*, we should get moving."

Jake pulled out a key card and swiped a pad next to a thick metal panel. The panel swung open with a teeth-jarring, creepy screech. Red lights played over Jake's face before the interior lit up a tablet computer on a charging station. He unplugged and removed the tablet and, using his shoulder, heaved the panel. It settled back in place with a resounding *clang.*

"Really?" Zoe asked. "A *tablet?*"

"If it weren't digital, we'd need a forklift. We better get going."

"Somebody needs to tell me what's going on."

"I guess that'll be Reaper when we get there, but if he's asking for *The Codex*, it can't be good."

If she'd been alarmed before, that statement scared the crap out of her. Considering what she'd done and seen as Death, that was saying something. But she could do nothing but meet this new challenge head on.

In moments, the duo strode through The Galatia House & Conference Spa in Huntsville, Alabama. Zoe wasn't sure how to interpret the "Conference Spa" part, but the people in the hotel meeting areas seemed relaxed and happy in their pop culture and punned t-shirts and button-festooned "Bags of Holding."

"Reaper's on the thirteenth floor." Jake had his phone out. The screen pulsed with a large red dot.

"I still can't believe you lo-jacked your own brother." Zoe said as a woman in an elaborate costume of leather and buckles sailed past with a whip-thin man in a *Flash* costume.

"All our calls and crews are geo-located now. For situations just like this."

Zoe suddenly detected a theme to the people around them. "I thought you said this *wasn't* one of your game things, Jake."

"It is and it isn't. This is a convention where there is game stuff, but so much more."

"Like that comic con thing you keep trying to tell me about?"

"Again yes and no. This one is run by fans, not companies looking for profit. It's smaller and more about the books, art, and stuff instead of the celebrity. Not that there's anything wrong with celebrity."

Zoe grinned. "It's so cute when you go into lecture mode. When was the last time you were at one of these?"

Jake sighed. "For fun? It's been a while. For business? A couple of years ago, we picked up an author known for *Star Wars* novels."

"You mean that Aaron guy from your book club? That's where you found him? I like him and Bob Aspirin. He's fun, too."

"Yeah, that's them. We can talk about that later." Jake held the elevator door open for her. "I've already received two texts and a voicemail from Reaper wanting to know where we are. I've never seen him like this."

They exited the elevator to find the hallway eerily silent and lined by more costumed and pop culture adorned people wearing convention badges. The line pointed to a room decorated in an *Addams' Family* motif.

"That's it. Room 1313."

"Perfect." as Zoe sailed past the convention-goers in the hallway, she did her best not to squirm. Their eyes followed Jake and Zoe's every move.

Just as they approached the room, Reaper stepped out, looking uncharacteristically rumpled and flustered. "Thank, well, everyone, you're finally here. You brought *The Codex*?"

Jake tapped the tablet. "Right here."

Reaper gestured toward the door. "After you."

Zoe led her chief soul collectors into the room.

"*YOU!*"

A short, curly-haired fireplug of a woman launched herself at Zoe's Ann Taylor black sharkskin blazer. "You bring him back!" She punctuated her words with sharp blows with balled fists. "You're *Death! Un-death* him! Right now!"

"Who is he?" Zoe's temper frayed a bit. She was tired of asking questions.

"He's my partner, my best friend, he's *ED!*"

"Ed?" Jake asked, perking up. "You mean *The Dravecky?*"

Zoe shot a helpless look at the body on the bed. "You know him?"

"Of him. He was a force in the fandom world."

Zoe gave the body more thorough study. Ed was a bear of a man in a convention logo t-shirt and jeans. His trimmed hair and beard lay neatly in place. "Wow. He really does look asleep."

"*Not* helping." Reaper pointed at the woman gaping at Zoe. "She won't let me near the soul."

"That's because you're not taking him!" the woman said. "Come on, Zoe, you can keep him here."

Zoe raised an index finger. "Stop. Just stop. First, Jake, is that even possible? Can we do that? And two, you. Who are you? And how do you know me?"

"Don't you remember? I *interviewed* you. I wrote under the name Skip...something. My name is Robyn. You pulled a horrible turn around on me, asking me how I wanted a loved one to die." She gestured toward Ed. "*This* wasn't...we didn't talk about any of this. So bring him back."

"I don't even know...there's only *one* entity I know who ever did that." Zoe hated feeling so out of the loop.

"Yeah, and He shared that 'gift' with his Son and the Apostles. He can share it with you." Robyn wasn't backing down.

"Yeah, and how do you think we ended up with this whole zombie craze? Coincidence? Don't think so. Jake, why aren't you saying anything?"

"I'm looking. I'm looking." His fingers flew across the surface of the tablet.

"That's why I asked him to bring *The Codex,*" Reaper said.

Zoe's exasperation level spiked. "Someone tell me what that tablet is this instant."

"It's the Rules for Death." Jake didn't even look up when he answered.

"I have *rules*? Since when?" Zoe felt oddly insulted.

"Since *always.*" Reaper and Jake said together.

Jake tapped the screen at a rapid pace. "Every Death *ever* has had rules to abide by. We generally guide you around most of the pitfalls. Okay, yeah, here it is. I'm so sorry, but this is in big, flashing red letters. No raising from the dead. No returning souls. We can't do it. Sorry, Skip."

"Robyn! And now I have to go over your head. Get Lynn on the phone. I want to talk to her."

Zoe's brain shorted out for a second. Robyn snatched the phone from Zoe's hand. And hit the call button. Disbelief resulted in a roar in Zoe's ears that blocked out most of what Robyn said. Then she handed the phone back. "Lynn wants to talk to you."

"Yes?"

"Here's what we're going to do." Lynn's voice was firm and newly distracted, and proceeded to rattle off a list of instructions.

"You're sure? Yes, ma'am." Zoe turned back to Reaper and Jake. "Get everyone off the floor. We're trying something...different."

Soon the thirteenth floor was deserted, attention diverted by EMTs bustling in and removing the body and the illusion of Robyn following behind. In the suite, Zoe and the Grimm Brothers stood by as Robyn confronted Ed's now-released soul.

"We have to go soon," Zoe said. "*She's* coming."

"Satan's not coming for him, is she?"

"No. She's coming for us." Reaper shuddered. "To make sure we finish the job."

"But"—Zoe's voice softened—"we can give you some time. Say goodbye. Let you have some closure."

Ed's soul shimmered in the translucent way most souls did, but with a golden glow. Zoe snapped her fingers, and the soul animated. "Let's give them some privacy."

The trio stood outside the hotel room door, hearing the rise and fall of voices in a wide variety of emotions. A new, brash voice and angry footfalls drowned out the voices in the room. Satan stormed down the hall with sparks striking off her flame-decorated drag queen boots.

"What are you three pansies doing out here? You have *one job*! One!" She poked Reaper in the gut with her trident. "You drag me out *on my night off?* You will pay. Now out of the way." She plowed through the door, while the trio hesitated.

"We're cowards," Zoe said.

"Yes, we are," Jake said.

"I prefer the term self-preservation." Reaper slumped

against the wall.

The door slammed back on its stops and Satan stormed out. "Okay, Ed's soul is ready. Don't call me like this again. Go do your damned jobs. And remember, hell to pay."

As soon as Satan's private elevator dinged, Zoe turned on the brothers. "Where's his assignment?"

"I've got it." Reaper clicked some commands on his phone and hers dinged. "That's what I have."

"Okay, let's get this done."

Robyn sprawled on the overstuffed, ugly armchair as Ed's soul hovered nearby. They both seemed worn and shell-shocked. Par for the course after an encounter with Satan. Zoe put on her best bedside manner and knelt by the chair.

"I'm sorry for your loss, Robyn, really, but we have to go now." Zoe checked her phone. "Ed's got a nice place by Tolkien. I'm told Sir Pratchett's moving in down the block. Jake and Reaper have a game night that Ed's welcome to join. We can talk jobs later, if he wants one with any of the Horsewomen."

"Wreak and Havoc will love this guy," Jake muttered.

Zoe shot him a look to shut up. "I think his place even backs up to Bunny's Hoppy Acres, and dogs are already lining up. Some Chow named Cain's been telling all the dogs something about hot dogs."

"Now the boys have to go. I'll take you to the hospital, and life will suck for a while, but you have friends and family. Neither you nor them are on my radar any time soon. I promise, Ed's in good hands."

"He'd better be. I have your number now." Robyn shook her fist at them all in a Scarlett O'Hara manner. "And don't you forget it."

Rhonda Eudaly lives in Arlington, Texas with her husband and two dogs. She's ventured into several industries and occupations for a wide variety of experience. She writes the part of Death (Zoe) in the *Four Redheads of the Apocalypse* books. She's the author of *Tarbox Station* and has short stories in several anthologies and other publications, most of which can be found on her website—www.RhondaEudaly.com.

Wainscoting's Folly
Tim Frayser

Dark clouds circled overhead as a Model T Ford chugged down the lonely country road. It went past an old oak tree and stopped at a barn in the middle of a field. Strange lights glowed in the twilight. A young man exited the vehicle carrying a small package. He passed some empty wooden casks and went inside.

Professor Azimuth Wainscoting busily watched a bank of dials and charts. He scowled at his assistant, Mortimer "Skippy" Skipworth, as the young man hurried into the improvised laboratory carrying a small package.

"Did you get the linseed oil?" the professor asked.

"You betcha, professor," Skippy said. "Well, sort of. The man at the store said you've already bought all the linseed oil in the county. All they had left was this pine-scented cleaner." He pulled the bottle out of the paper sack and pointed to the label. "It's mostly linseed oil."

"It will have to do!" said the professor. "Pour it into the vat!" Skippy stood on his tippy toes and poured the contents of the bottle into a large cauldron labeled "input." Clouds of steam swirled around the room as a small generator making a put-put-put sound drove a series of wheels and pulleys.

The professor looked around his laboratory with pride. "This last batch should complete the process!"

"Professor," said Skippy, discarding the empty bottle, "what is all this?"

"The future of mankind!" cried the professor. "I am creating a power source unrivaled in human history! And the beauty of it all is that it centers on one of nature's simplest products... linseed oil!"

"Uh," said Skippy, scratching his head. "I don't get it."

The professor stood up, his white lab coat flowing dramatically behind him. "For centuries, mankind has been fascinated with phlogiston, the combustible material within all matter. Efforts to fully understand phlogiston have been frustrated by the fact that the material has no mass."

Skippy frowned. "Wait, hold on, phlogiston? Wasn't

phlogiston theory discredited by the scientific community back in the eighteenth century?"

"Fools!" cried the professor. "They had no idea of the power they so casually dismissed!"

"Does this have something to do with that strange magnet you invented last week?" Skippy asked.

"That was simply one step in the process," the professor explained. "The phlogiston attractionator attracts phlogiston from explosive material, true, but here's no point in attracting something that has no mass! That was when I needed to find a stable medium."

Skippy took a hard look at the apparatus around him. The input cauldron emptied into a long graduated cylinder, which was set between the aforementioned phlogiston attractionator and a waist-high pile of black residue in the middle of the room. The pile of sooty material looked suspiciously like gunpowder. The cylinder itself emptied into a twenty-gallon steel drum.

Skippy wiped a smudge of the black dust off on his trousers as he collected his thoughts. "Have you been extracting the kinetic combustible phlogiston from all this gunpowder and storing it in linseed oil?"

"Of course," said the professor. "My research has concluded that pure linseed oil has, above all other substances, the ability to store extracted phlogiston. It's completely safe!"

Skippy looked around the laboratory. There were at least a dozen twenty-gallon drums lined up against the walls. "Are all these drums full of linseed oil?"

"Phlogistonated linseed oil!" the professor said proudly. "The linseed oil in those barrels is saturated with combustible phlogiston. I believe I shall call it... phlogistonglycerin! Or perhaps Wainscottingite! The power stored here will revolutionize the world!"

"Professor, you're mad!" yelled Skippy. "It's too unstable! The mixture is too powerful! It goes against the laws of nature!"

"Nature, schmature!" cried the professor. "The world will soon recognize my greatness, my genius, for I am Professor Azimuth Wain—!"

No one ever saw Professor Wainscoting or Skippy again. Witnesses later testified the explosion was very bright and could be heard miles away.

One wheel was all they ever found of the Model T. The old oak tree was knocked over by the blast. The crater it left behind was thirty yards across and, for some reason, seemed to be... pine-scented.

FIN

Tim Frayser has been telling stories his whole life. After retiring from the City of Tulsa, he now works at the Tulsa Zoo, where he sometimes gets to drive the train. For the past several years, he has volunteered as a Black Rock Ranger at the annual Burning Man festival. He is a photographer, martial artist, cartoonist, writer and zealous traveler. Tim's first publication was *The Necronomicrap* from Yard Dog Press. His novel, *Memoirs of an Ex-Zombie*, is available from Amazon.com.

My Addiction
James Hollaman

I thought I could quit and I tried, I really did. I started taking care of myself. Was clean for over a year. That all ended when I saw my dealers on the corner near where I work.

I had just stepped out for lunch and was on my way back when I saw them. The entire gang was there, wearing their colors. They were calling out to people, trying to reel them in. Sadly, I saw other addicts forking out money for product that would not even last them the night. I knew this because it would never have lasted for me.

I forced myself back to work. I figured if I could just work my way past the craving for a fix that it would go away. It didn't. My concentration turned to crap. I could not focus on anything.

After a few lost sales, my boss let me go home early. I walked down the street in a daze. I found myself standing in front of the group with my money in my hand. Tried to talk myself out of buying.

In the end they won.

Damn you Girl Scouts and your Thin Mints...

James Hollaman has stories in three of the *Bubbas of the Apocalypse* anthologies—*International House of Bubbas*, *Houston We've Got Bubbas!*, and *A Bubba In Time Saves None*. He also has a story in *Flush Fiction I*, and *I Didn't Quite Make It To Oz.*

Jimmy did the cover art for *The Bubba Chronicles, Marking the Signs and Other Tales of Mischief*, and *I Didn't Quite Make It To Oz* in addition to the art on the back cover of this volume.

He is always creating.

He also runs a "small" convention party called Room Con.

Princess in Boots

Trina Jacobs

"Exactly how stupid are you?" the grey tabby said to the miller's third son.

Jack gave the cat a puzzled look and worked his jaw as he tried to come up with a response. "I don't know," he said, fishing out a lump of earwax and studying it intently.

The cat paced back and forth along between a set of wagon ruts. "That damn miller couldn't have a picked a worse time to die," she muttered.

"But, Puss," Jack said, "maybe if you hadn't pushed him—"

The cat glared at the young man. "Don't call me 'Puss,'" she snarled.

"But you're a cat," Jack said, "and all cats are called 'Puss.'"

"I've already told you, I'm not a real cat. I'm under a curse."

Jack looked confused.

"Don't you know that cats can't talk?"

"But you're a cat, Puss, and you've been talking all day."

The tabby rolled her emerald eyes. "My name is Princess Yvonna." She sat daintily on the grass between the ruts, lifted a fine white forepaw to her face, and proceeded to wash it with delicate pink tongue. "Of course," she said, pausing without looking up, "you may also address me as 'Your Royal Highness.'"

"Whatever you say, Puss," Jack said.

The princess stopped bathing. Her forepaw remained in the air as she gave Jack a chilling gaze. He would have shrunk away from it, if he'd been looking at her, instead staring off toward a distant field. "There are so many kinds of cows," he muttered. "Cows with spots. Cows without spots." The possibilities were endless.

Her Royal Highness startled Jack from his reverie by sinking her claws deeply into his calf. He shrieked and jumped backwards, imagining a herd of tiny horned cows goring him. He didn't know whether or not they had spots.

Princess Yvonna shook her royal head as she sat watching him. "I knew I should have gone with the middle son."

Jack looked around, there were no killer cows in sight. Not even little tiny ones. There was only Puss, who stared at him with a look of contempt, just the way his father, brothers, and the villagers did. It made him feel better.

"I need a pair of boots," the cat-princess said.

Jack scratched his head. "Boots? Cats don't wear boots."

Princess Yvonna sighed. "How many talking cats do you know?"

The young man's face screwed up in confusion. After a minute or so, his expression brightened and he said, "One!" He paused. "But why do you need boots?"

"All talking cats wear boots," the princess said, starting towards the village.

That made as much sense to Jack as most things did, which wasn't very much. He followed the cat to a shop with a sign in the shape of a shoe.

"Why does your cat need boots?" the shoemaker asked, brows furrowed.

"She's a talking cat," Jack said, grinning.

The cobbler glanced at Princess Yvonna. "A talking cat?"

"Yup."

"And she needs boots because...?"

"She's a talking cat."

The shoemaker put his hands on his hips. "And?"

"All talking cats wear boots."

"Who told you this?"

"She did," Jack said, indicating the cat.

"If I make boots for your cat, will you leave my shop and never come back?"

Princess Yvonna nodded.

Jack said, "Yes."

As he turned away, the shoemaker mumbled, "He must have eaten those magic beans again."

As they left the shop, the princess wrinkled her kitty nose and said, "Jack, it's time for your yearly bath."

Jack pouted.

"I know an excellent place for bathing," the cat said. "People who bathe there only have to do it annually."

Jack had no clue what 'annually' meant. "There aren't any cows in there, are there?" he asked, giving the tabby a suspicious glare.

"Cows?" She hesitated. "No. No cows."

They soon arrived at the pond. "Take your clothes off and get in," the cat said.

Jack stripped and touched a toe to the water and turned to the princess, "It's freezing!"

The cat gave him the evil eye.

He backed to the edge of the pond and kept going, then fell in with a mighty splash.

Just then, a fine carriage rumbled down the alleged road. "Don't say a word!" the enchanted princess said.

Princess Yvonna hid among the reeds and bushes beside the pond. "Help! Help!" she cried, then she turned to Jack and muttered, "Splash."

The carriage stopped. King Bob the Mediocre peered out.

Jack stared at the royal carriage through the brush.

"Splash!" hissed the princess.

His Majesty surveyed the area. "What sort of assistance do you require?"

"Robbers attacked my carriage and stole it!" Princess Yvonna said.

"And you are?"

"A princess!"

"And you need rescuing?" His Royal Mediocrity said, frowning. He'd never been very good at rescuing princesses and was somewhat out of practice, what with the paperwork his position required.

"Yes! Please, Sire, they took my horses, jewels, and clothes—"

The king's face brightened. He even smiled. "Took your clothes, huh?"

"They threw me in the water and tried to drown me!"

The bushes rustled as Jack hauled himself out of the water. "Stay down!" the cat hissed, "you don't want the king to see you naked, do you?"

Jack shook his head violently.

"Wet and naked," leered the king.

"Please, Your Majesty, I need some clothes, and my fiancé will be worried about me. I could really use a ride to his castle. It's not very far."

"It would be my pleasure to escort you," King Bob said, sounding very kingly.

"Clothes?"

The king cleared his throat. "Oh, yeah. That too."

Everyone knew that ever since she'd learned to drive a team of horses, the King's daughter had practically lived in the royal carriage. She was a messy girl and the carriage didn't have a maid.

King Bob ordered a royal coach-flunky to sort through the mess and find an outfit for the princess. The servant took a deep breath and held it as he opened the carriage door. The king was up to his knees in women's clothes, papers, junk mail, and fast food containers.

The servant threw some various and assorted items of feminine attire to the bushes where Jack and the princess hid.

"Go ahead, put them on," Princess Yvonna said.

Jack stared at her.

"You won't be allowed to ride in the king's carriage with me if you don't get dressed."

Jack studied a feminine undergarment. It looked even more complicated than his tunic and breeches. "Do I have to wear all this?"

"Yes. Remember those thieves I mentioned?"

Jack nodded slowly.

"They stole your clothes."

At long last, Jack appeared decked out in his new finery. It included a large floppy hat. This was a good thing. King Bob and his servants stared at him with wide eyes and open mouths.

"No wonder the thieves tried to drown her," the king said to his men. "It would have been a mercy killing."

"Remember, no talking to the king," the cat said. "That's my job."

"Where is your fiancé waiting for you?" King Bob's face was greenish and his voice weak.

"Castle Giantuglyogre," the cat said from behind Jack's voluptuous skirts.

Jack was too frightened to tremble. He'd heard of Castle Giantuglyogre. A giant ugly ogre lived there!

"Get over it, Jack," the princess hissed.

Jack heaved himself into the carriage, knocking down the coachman and two servants in the process. Princess Yvonna slipped in gracefully and found a relatively clean place to curl up while all eyes were on Jack.

Jack sat across from King Bob and smiled at him with a vapid look on his face.

The king couldn't take his eyes off Jack. Jack thought it was because he looked so pretty. He was wrong.

King Bob never said a word to Jack, but every now and then, he stuck his head out of the window and shouted, "Can't those horses run any faster?"

"If they'd gotten a look at this princess, they'd be running for their lives," the coachman grumbled.

When Castle Giantuglyogre appeared around a bend in the road, King Bob took hold of Jack's arm in a courtly manner, kicked the door open, and shoved the fake princess out. The coachman never slowed the horses.

Jack landed face first with his butt in the air. Princess Yvonna leapt deftly from the speeding coach and landed on the young man's backside with only her unbooted forelegs gripping his skirts. By the time Jack lifted himself out of the dirt, King Bob and his entourage were well out of sight.

Princess Yvonna and Jack walked through the gate in an adorable white picket fence and approached the castle.

"Oh no," Jack said, "the drawbridge is closed. How will we get in?"

"The drawbridge shouldn't be a problem since there isn't a moat."

Jack still looked confused.

"We'll go in that way," the princess said, pointing with a forepaw. Beside the drawbridge was a door. A screen door, propped open by a lawn chair.

A handsome young man sat alone at a trestle table in the castle's great hall losing at solitaire.

Princess Yvonna cleared her throat in a regal manner. The young man jumped up, knocking the bench over. Then he got a look at Jack. He fell backwards and tripped over the fallen bench.

"I am Princess Yvonna. I'm here to see my fiancé, Prince Gunther Giantuglyogre."

The tall aristocratic young man stared at Jack, his face frozen in horror. "He's not here! He died! He's out of town! He's already married!"

"You must be Gunther," the cat said.

The man shook his head violently. "No-no-no-no-no-no—"

"You are not dead, married, and/or out of town," the princess said. "I'd know a Giantuglyogre anywhere."

Jack screeched, "A giant ugly ogre!" He lifted his skirts and minced in place, searching the nearly empty hall for a hiding place.

Prince Gunther snorted, crossed his arms, stuck his lower lip out in an impressive pout. "So you're my fiancée, Princess Yvonna," he said, starring at Jack.

"Hey! Over here!" the cat said, stepping forward. "I'm Princess Yvonna."

Prince Gunther looked mortified. "I am not marrying a cat. That wasn't in the contract."

"I'm not really a cat, you idiot. A nasty old hag put a curse on me."

The prince's face turned bright red. He studied his bootlaces and swallowed hard. "Was it my Aunt Edna?"

"Who else? That witch doesn't think any princess is good enough for her 'wittle Gunthie.'"

"I hate it when she does this." Prince Gunther shuffled his feet and kept his head down.

"How do you think I feel?" the princess asked.

"I suppose the spell has to be broken in the usual way, with a kiss?" the prince asked, apparently addressing a large dust bunny.

"Pucker up, big boy," Princess Yvonna said, removing her tiny boots.

Jack watched swallows fly among the rafters and thought about how pretty he felt in his new dress.

Prince Gunther strode boldly across the room, swept Jack into his arms, and gave him a big 'Oklahoma hello', even though Oklahoma hadn't been invented yet.

Jack kissed the prince back. With tongue. Prince Gunther dropped Jack to the floor, where he stayed, watching little birdies, stars, and tiny cows fly around his head.

The prince coughed, hacked, spit, and wiped his mouth.

Princess Yvonna stood beside Prince Gunther in her true form, that of a beautiful human princess. She looked down at her outfit and cried, "This dress is out of style! It's from last year and I was only a cat for a month! I'll get Aunt Edna for this!"

Jack thought her dress was pretty. Almost as pretty as his.

The princess grabbed her prince by the upper arm and dragged him across the great hall. "I am not changing my name to Giantuglyogre," she said, as she hauled her fiancé out of the room.

"Yes, dear," Prince Gunther said.

After a few minutes, the little stars, birdies, and cows went away, so Jack took a nap on the cold stone floor. He'd slept in worse places. Eventually, he wandered back to the village, where he was soon known not only as the village idiot, but also as the kingdom idiot.

Princess Yvonna and Prince Gunther married and lived happily ever after. Or at least Princess Yvonna did.

Trina Jacobs was born on Halloween. Her friends say that explains a lot. She grew up in upstate NY where there are four seasons, but three of them are winter. She currently lives near Tulsa, OK, where there is much less snow, with three dogs, a cat, a horse, and her husband.

Dark Noise

vck (vickey malone kennedy)

A horrible racket, like a dragon clawing through a concrete wall, echoed through the house. I assumed we had squirrels in the attic, again. An under panel had blown off the awning during the last thunderstorm. It left a gap large enough for a toddler to crawl through.

I didn't want animals living in my attic, but I certainly did not want to be the one to go up there and flush them out. I couldn't afford an exterminator. Sadly, Child Protective Services frowns on shoving small children through holes in the roof in search of four footed trespassers.

A squirrel in the rafters migrates to the lower levels of the building sooner or later. The little buggers seem to thrive on the peanut butter flavored rat poison I sprinkle in the loft. The gnawing grew louder. My daughter grew too terrified to sit idly by waiting to be eaten by the monster devouring everything in its path; judging by the consistent chomping.

Using the flashlight app on my cell phone, I tiptoed toward the kitchen, like a drunken teen sneaking into the house after curfew. Myriah crept through the dining room behind me, clinging to the back of my shirt. We followed the scraping sound, searched for its origin with the pale beam of light, and tripped across the cluttered room.

Myriah's frantic breath blew wispy waves of hair across my neck, and sent cold chills down my spine. I wanted to tell her to calm down and back the F off, but we were trying so hard— and failing so miserably—to be quiet. We didn't want to scare away the intruder before we had a chance to apprehend him.

Actually, I would have been perfectly happy if the varmint vanished like a frightened little dormouse. I had no desire to come face to face with some beady eyed, sharp toothed, cat sized, rodent in the dark. But, Myriah insisted we hunt down the carnivorous creature and stomp it into the ground.

Ice cubes clanked out of the ice maker and clanged into the ice bucket. Myriah jumped forward, crashed into me, and sent us both sprawling, face down, on the floor.

We squealed like preschoolers. I dropped the phone. The light disappeared.

We made enough commotion to scare away any prowling predator poking around the pantry. Crawling on hands and knees, we searched for the phone. Myriah found it, tried to hand it to me, and elbowed me right in the face. I licked the coppery taste of blood from my lip.

When our squeals finally faded, the disturbing rustling resumed. The scratching was so close to my left ear I could hear the beast breathing, and smell its nutty breath.

We scrambled to our feet and jumped backwards. We collided, stumbled, and fell. I landed in her lap. She pushed me off, and shoved me forward. I kicked an ice chest sitting beside the refrigerator, knocked it over, and dumped a brown paper sack to the floor.

The bag rattled, emitted the rumblings of a mountain lion emerging from a cave, and then quieted.

I fumbled with the icons on the phone screen. A pinpoint of light flashed into the dark cavernous container. It reflected off two bright red orbs moving toward the mouth of the sack, and then flickered off again.

We tried to regain our footing, but only managed to half scoot, half crawl backwards across the kitchen. The crunching sound moved toward our piercing screams.

Overhead light flooded the pitch black room.

"What the hell is all the screaming about?" asked my son, his hand still poised over the switch on the wall. "Y'all need to keep it down in here. I'm trying to play video games."

The bag shook and rattled. The demon remained hidden inside its paper sanctuary. Myriah and I screamed, again.

Ian bent down, picked up the sack, and stuck his hand inside.

"Don't! Stop!" Myriah and I yelled in unison. "It might bite."

He pulled out a fat, fanged, fist of fur, stuck it up to his nose, Eskimo kissed it, and laughed. "Thanks for finding my ferret, Mom. I've been looking for her for a week."

–end–

vck (vickey malone kennedy) writes Science Fiction, Fantasy, Paranormal Romance, and Erotica. She is the 2011 winner of the Darrell Award for Best Midsouth Short Story, "Bobbie Sue Almost Got Married" in *A Bubba In Time Saves None* published by Yard Dog Press.

Originally from Alamo, Tennessee, vck now lives in Norman, Oklahoma with her ever growing brood of grandchildren.

The Troll in Tower Grove Park
Zoanne Leavy

I'm always the last to hear everything. There is no bit of news that comes to me when it occurs or even shortly thereafter. I am the woman who never knows what is going on. When Dave broke up with Emily, I didn't hear about it until I asked Kara if we shouldn't be thinking about some sort of shower for Emily. Kara looked at me pityingly and said, "Sweetie, they broke up in April. Didn't you hear about it?" Then there was the time at work when I heard that Curt and his entire team were being laid off. "How horrible," I said to Andy. He looked at me like I was an alien. "Where have you been? We all knew it was in the works for the last two months." So it was no different when I finally heard about the disappearing dogs.

Now, I see my neighbors on a pretty regular basis. We don't do the block party thing, but people are to-ing and fro-ing a lot and we tend to see each other at least weekly and stop for a little chat. We are, I think, a reasonably intelligent and well-behaved bunch. It's a quiet neighborhood, just across the street from Tower Grove Park, with nicely maintained houses and four-plexes. I live in one of the apartments, and I would venture to say that I fit in well with our little community.

So I was quite surprised, and, well, truthfully a little miffed, to discover that I had not heard anything about disappearing dogs. The first I heard was from Frank. He and his partner, Eric are a lovely couple who live in the house next door to my building. I was hauling some groceries out of the car, when I saw Frank come around the side of his house with the garden hose.

"Hey, Frank, do you have a sec to help me get this to the front door?" I hate running back and forth, and even though I try to keep my shopping under control, I sometimes end up with more bags than I can carry in one trip.

"Sure. Be right there." Frank made sure the hose wasn't twisted, then draped in over the metal railing by the steps and came over to assist. As we dropped the bags inside the door, I heard Cherie, their Pomeranian, yipping in the back yard.

"Thanks, Frank. You're a pal. Sounds like Cherie has found a squirrel."

"She's very unhappy with us. We've been leaving her in the back yard when she needs to go out and she feels she's missing something in the neighborhood." He peeked around the corner of the porch to check on her.

"Don't you usually take her for a run in the Park? Which reminds me I need to get back on my walking schedule." So much for my New Year's resolution to walk daily, or at least five times a week. I hadn't strolled through the Park in over two months. My bad.

"We haven't taken her over there for a few weeks." Frank looked over at the Park like it was the Haunted Forest in some fairy tale. "Ever since the dogs have gone missing...."

"Missing dogs?" Oh, yeah. I was right on top of things again. "Who's missing? What happened?"

"Oh," Frank looked at me in surprise. "Hadn't you heard?"

I sighed loudly.

"I think it started a few weeks ago. You know how a lot of people like to walk their dogs in the evening, and there's always a few who let their puppies off the leash."

I nodded, trying to look like I knew where this story was going.

"Well," he continued, looking back at the Park, "somebody lost their dog and couldn't find him. Then a few days later, someone from over on Shaw lost their terrier. Then it was someone else who lives on Shenandoah lost a poodle, I think it was a poodle. Might have been a doodle. Anyway, I'm seeing all these signs up for lost dogs and I said to Eric, 'we need to keep an eye on Cherie when we walk her.' So he makes this stupid joke about checking the Chinese restaurants on Grand. I'm thinking these people are just stupid to let their dogs off the leash. Even the best-behaved dog is going to run off if they see a squirrel or catch a scent. And then I talked to Bruce. You know Bruce, he lives about two blocks down that way..." He gestured vaguely to the north. "...has...*had*...a Chihuahua. I ran into him putting up signs on the poles, looking for Marie Claire. He looked awful, like he hadn't slept in days, eyes all red. He's telling me he had Marie Claire on her leash. He was sitting on one of the benches in the Park. Had his eyes closed, trying to mediate and find his center, as he put it. Apparently he'd just had a fight with Simon and was trying to calm down.

Anyway, Marie Claire was yapping at everything, like they do, and he just sat there with his eyes closed, doing breathing exercises and wishing she'd be quiet. He said he felt her pull on the leash, then she stopped and got quiet. He sat for a few more minutes, becoming one with the universe or whatever, then opened his eyes and got up to walk on. That's when he noticed he was holding a leash with no dog on the other end." Pausing for effect, Frank brushed his brown locks dramatically back from his face.

"Gee," I observed, "you wouldn't think she could break loose from her lead like that."

Frank flipped his wrist and pointed a finger at me. "Well, here's the surprise. According to Bruce, the lead was intact. The clasp was still in one piece and he swears someone must have come up behind him, unhooked her, and stolen the dog." He paused again for more effect and then added, "I can't believe you haven't heard any of this."

That's right, Frank, I thought. Rub it in. "So, has anyone reported it to the police? It sounds like a dog-napping ring to me."

Frank waved his hand at me, then placed it palm down on his chest. Did I mention that Frank is theatrical? "Oh, heavens, yes. Some of those animals were quite valuable. But do you think the local constabulary could be interested enough to move off their hefty bottoms for anything as mundane as a dog? You remember last year, when we couldn't even get them to investigate the break-ins three blocks over. Roger Eastman was the block captain and he was livid! He got people to send emails to the mayor and the aldermen, but you know our alderman is just worthless."

When Frank paused for breath, I jumped in. "So no one has investigated? What about the Neighborhood Watch? Isn't Marge Branson in charge of that? She never misses an opportunity to get everyone involved."

Frank peered around the porch toward his back yard again. "Oh, yes. There's a meeting tomorrow night. Didn't you get the flyer? I've got to get Cherie in before she has time to mat up her fur in those bushes. Eric and I will walk down to the meeting with you. I think it starts at 7:30. See you."

With that Frank bounded down off the porch and headed down the gangway. "Cherie, get out of the bushes. If I have to spend another hour combing you, you are going to be one sorry Pom." His back gate clanked shut, and I stood there and stared at the Park.

I won't go into all the details of the meeting. As might be expected, it was chaotic, dramatic, and over-blown for almost two hours. Finally, after I had exhibited extreme self-control in not throttling at least two of my neighbors (yes, Ricardo, I mean you and Victor), a sort of plan was developed. Several of us agreed to wander through the Park between dusk and closing and see if we could pinpoint anything suspicious. I, of course, volunteered. Mainly since Eric is always pointing out that I'm not involved enough in the community efforts. Just because I announced I would be out of town in May when they did the Neighborhood Spruce Up Weekend. Sweeping alleys is not my thing, and I really did intend to visit my cousin in Joliet, but then he decided to take that weekend to go to the Bahamas. So I planned to "vacation" at home, but Frank saw me sneaking out with the kitty litter.

So we were three nights into the plan when the next dog got snatched. I had the 7 p.m. to 9 p.m. shift and was just meeting up with Dakota, who had the same shift, but the opposite end of the Park. We agreed that nothing untoward had occurred when we heard a shriek. I admit, I don't run as fast as I used to. The knees are the first to go, or maybe they're the second. Anyway, Dakota, who is younger and a couple of pounds lighter, I might add, took off and she got to the hysterical woman about a minute before I did. It was a familiar story. The woman was reading her Nook, sitting quietly with her dog, and when she got up to leave, the leash was empty and the dog was gone. Dakota and I pulled out our flashlights and started looking and calling for the dog, whose name was Snookie. Apparently the lady was from New Jersey. Dakota had the presence of mind to pull out her cell and call her hubby to round up some of the Watch to help with the search. She headed south and I headed towards the Lily Pond, calling for the missing animal. I got no response except for a slovenly individual lying on one of the benches who called out "I'll be your Snookie, baby doll." Tempting though it was to demonstrate that I was not his baby doll, I moved on, focused on my mission.

Shortly, I heard other voices calling, but nothing to indicate the animal had been found. My night vision isn't particularly good, so after almost a half an hour I headed back to where the distraught lady was sobbing into someone's shoulder. There were about ten other members of the Watch standing around, and it seemed everyone was arguing about where they had searched, who hadn't searched, and how this had happened when the patrol was in the area. I'll admit I was feeling a bit guilty about the snatch occurring on my watch, but since we had no eyewitness accounts, we didn't really know what to look for.

So after some more arguing, four people agreed to get their cars and drive around the perimeter of the park, then through the interior roads. The rest of us picked a direction, with the intent of walking and searching until we reached the boundary of the park. I had planned to head north in the direction of my apartment, but Frank and Eric had already taken that section. So I grudgingly went south instead.

Swinging the flashlight back and forth as I went, I felt fairly certain I wasn't going to find anything. Whoever was doing this was a professional. They were careful, quiet, and had a quick escape route. It was probably time to get the animal rights groups involved and stage a sit-in in the Mayor's office. I was brightening at the thought of the Mayor's horrified face as he surveyed a group of animal lovers packing his waiting area, when I heard a noise. It wasn't a bark, but it wasn't a sound I could readily identify and I stopped short to listen. Silence. Just as I was convinced I was hearing things, it repeated. This time it sounded more like a muffled belch. Great, I thought to myself, I've stumbled on a wino hiding in the bushes.

With some caution, I continued down the path, which meandered between some tall bushes. On the other side was a small streamlet with a picturesque wooden bridge crossing over. The stream never had much water in it unless there was a good-sized storm. This had been a very wet spring, so I wasn't surprised to see that the banks had been heavily cut away. The bridge was still secure but you could see that there was much more room underneath than there had been the previous year.

The moon was about half-full and rising into the treetops, so I took a moment to stand on the bridge and stare at the dance of moonlight and shadows. I had just made the decision to move on, when I heard a scuffling noise beneath me. Naturally, my first thought was that I had disturbed one of the occasional raccoons that we knew frequented the trash cans. However, the scuffling was followed by a low, back-of-the-throat growl. Definitely not a raccoon. Now I was torn between running for my life from a rabid animal, or instead putting some distance between myself and the bridge, then flashing my light to see what was under there.

I opted for quietly crossing the bridge and moving a ways downstream. It did occur to me that I might yell for assistance since there were certainly other members of the patrol within hearing, but I also knew I would never live down the interminable jokes if it turned out to be something like a hormonal cat. So, clutching the flashlight tightly in hand, I shone the light into the darkness beneath the bridge.

Glowing red eyes reflected back at me and I was not encouraged. Then the eyes blinked. Then they tilted slightly to one side, as if the creature was cocking its head at me. For some reason, this made me feel slightly better. I held my ground, and, because I obviously wasn't thinking clearly, I said "Hello."

The eyes blinked again and whatever it was seemed to move a bit closer to the side of the bridge. Then another movement brought it further into the light, but now the eyes were squinting. Feeling it was the polite thing to do, I tilted the light downward so it wasn't directly in the creature's eyes. This seemed to encourage the creature to move a bit further from under the bridge.

Now I got a much better look, between the flashlight and the moonlight. Staring back at me was an extremely furry (or perhaps long-haired) being with very large red eyes, an unfortunate overbite, stubby body, and long arms that ended in finger-like claws. TROLL! my mind shrieked, although how in blazes I had any idea what a troll looked like, I have no idea. Still crouching, I wanted to run madly for safety, but I was strangely frozen in place.

Perhaps sensing my discomfort, the TROLL! dropped back on his pudgy butt with a noisy plop. He (alright, it could have been a female, I couldn't see anything to tell me exactly what the gender was) continued to stare at me, and after a moment, made a soft "Grrrgle" at me. I took this to be a friendly comment. He shifted slightly, probably because he was sitting on some sharp gravel, and I saw something glint lightly behind him. Staring harder, I decided that what I was looking at was the collar and tag from one of the unfortunate missing dogs.

Daylight dawns on Marblehead, as one of my friends often says. Here was the reason for the missing animals. This strange creature was obviously just hungry. My mind ran through a number of possibilities, trying to make some sense of this all. And not succeeding very well. He was a mythical animal. He was in our park. He was eating dogs. He was clever enough to stay out of sight. He didn't seem to wish to threaten people. He wasn't real. He was sitting in front of me, now scratching his belly as I tried to process. The only conclusion I could come to was that this TROLL! wasn't really a danger to me, he probably didn't know how he had come to be here either, and he might only want to live and let live. Two sides of my mind were having a battle royal trying to explain what was obviously here, when it couldn't possibly be here. My head started to ache.

Eventually, I came around to the conclusion that we had a TROLL! in the park. This TROLL! was eating people's pets and that was not acceptable. I could call Animal Control but I felt rather strongly that such a call would be followed by a visit from the Mental Health people. And if I could get someone to believe me, less enlightened souls might be more inclined to shoot the poor thing first and dissect him later. My moral compass jerked wildly at the thought. No, somehow I was going to have to keep him a secret, and change his diet. Right.

Feeling rather light-headed from all this cogitation, I decided to make a move and see what happened. Perhaps a good night's sleep would prove this was just some kind of hallucination, brought on perhaps by bad sushi. I stood slowly. The TROLL! continued to watch me with interest. I took a step back. The TROLL! scratched at his ear, ruffling his grayish fur. I waved in a genial manner and took another step back and began to turn away. Then he moved. But after my heart nearly jumped out of my chest, I realized that he was just rolling himself back under the bridge.

The confrontation ended, I walked back toward the apartment, wondering just what in the blazes I was going to do about all this. As you might have gathered, I'm a very big, uh, make that enthusiastic, animal lover. I have cats. I play with all the dogs on my street. I make stupid cooing noises at puppies and kittens. And in my mind, this TROLL was just another animal, and although it appeared he might have the ability to rip my arm off and beat me over the head with it, he just didn't seem to be threatening. More like an animal that is lost and confused and just trying to make the best of things. I sighed heavily and asked the Universe for enlightenment.

And there it was. As I arrived at my place, Frank and Eric were just getting out of their car, carrying several bags.

Frank waved cheerily and called, "We got hungry after wandering all over the park and decided to get some dinner from Arturo's on the Hill. They messed up the order, so we got a free order of toasted ravioli. Do you want it?"

The Universe apparently had take-out. "Thanks, Frank. I'll take you up on that." I hurried over to take the box from them and then turned back to the park. "Hey," Frank called, "aren't you done with your patrol in the park? It's getting pretty late."

"No prob," I called back to him. "Just thought I'd snack in the moonlight. Never know what you're going to see."

"Silly girl," Eric responded, and I set off for the bridge.

So in no time, I was leaving an open box of toasted ravs just below the bridge and waiting to see what happened. Slowly, a furry paw (hand?) came out and reached into the box. It withdrew with a ravioli. Chewing noises followed and the hand returned to the box. After it appeared to be empty, there was a rustling of leaves, and a head poked back out into the moonlight. The red eyes regarded me again, and then I saw something that I swear was a smile appear as his lips curved up over the pointy teeth. A loud belch followed, perhaps part of a Troll custom to indicate enjoyment.

And that's how I solved the mystery of the disappearing dogs, discovered a mythical creature, and came to have a standing order at Arturo's for an order of ravioli on a daily basis. They have kindly offered me a discount for larger orders, so it's not as pricy as I feared. Meanwhile, I am sticking to my exercise schedule of a daily walk in the park. Frank and Eric are very impressed with my will-power. Which brings me to the downside of this whole thing.

I can't tell anyone about the troll. For once, in my entire life of being three steps behind in the important news and gossip, I cannot tell my story. I can't be ahead of the curve for just once. I have a story that would set the entire neighborhood back on its collective heels, and I can't. Say. A. Thing.

Damn!

I can only hope that I have the fortitude, when next someone looks at me sadly and says "Oh, didn't you hear about that", to refrain from speaking, and maybe just resort to biting them on the ankle instead. I may have picked that up from my friend.

Zoanne Leavy is a proud member of the Yard Dog crew, and you can find her work in *Houston: We've Got Bubbas!* and *I Didn't Quite Make It to Oz*. Besides science fiction and fantasy, she also delves (not a euphemism) into erotica. See *The Mammoth Book of the Kama Sutra*. Currently she is leading the Pro Liaison/Programming Team for Archon. Never let it be said that she doesn't take on challenges. Oh, and she enjoys research ("Now, how do you get your leg into that position?"). Current works in progress are one short story, two novellas, a novel, and a new project—a history of her family's radio station.

Salvage
William Ledbetter

Sharpie scanned the north side of the abandoned factory complex through dust caked windows, but saw nothing moving. If anyone approached from the direction of the city, she should see them coming up Johnson Road and would have plenty of time to hide. The doors and windows on the south side were all still intact and locked, so intruders entering from that direction would have to break in and would hopefully make some noise.

Her breath fogged the window, so she moved further back and closer to Kitty. The robot didn't generate a lot of heat, but every little bit helped. With cold-numbed fingers she felt around inside the pouch hanging at her side, but found nothing. Dried peas was the only food she could afford, but even those were long gone. She sighed and looked back into the gloomy factory interior, but she saw nothing moving. The machines had been looted long ago, but the floors, walls and workbenches were still littered with interesting debris—some of which people even bought—but she hated the factories. They were too dark and spooky. She leaned against Kitty. She knew the boxy machine wasn't a real cat, but it moved, made noises and was warm.

Almost as a response to that thought, Kitty gave a faint beep indicating she'd finished scanning. Sharpie named the file the exact words from the front of the manual—careful to get the caps and punctuation right—then hit transmit and sent it to the servers in the market, where her customer could purchase it. She removed another stack of paper from the ring binder. She slipped the fragile, yellowed sheets into Kitty's hopper, patted her scarred hide and hit scan. The paper was wrinkled and frayed around the edges, so Kitty took extra time gently examining each sheet with probes and before lifting it on a puff of air and pulling it into the scanner. She'd ruined too many with the ancient tractor feed.

Sharpie pulled the old marker from her pocket, opened the cap and put a black mark on her finger. It still worked. That made her smile. She replaced the cap and traced her finger along the pretty script on its side.

A scuffling sound came from about three yards behind her. She spun around, almost dropping the marker as she put Kitty between her and the stranger. They had come to almost grabbing distance! Her heart thudded in her chest. She wanted to run, but hated to leave Kitty.

The woman held hands away from her body in the way adults always did when they didn't want to appear threatening to children or animals. Sharpie knew that was a lie. That's how she'd been caught the first time and it wasn't going to work again.

"Are you Sharpie?"

Sharpie flinched. How did this woman know her name?

"Please don't run. I've been looking for you."

That made the hairs on Sharpie's neck stand up. She hadn't told anyone in the market. The women didn't look like a slave catcher, she was too well groomed and wore a clean, one-piece coverall that looked like a uniform, but that could be a ploy.

"Who're you?" Sharpie said.

"My name is Danita Sanchez," she said with a slight smile. "You might recognize me better from my email address, airhog776@nasa.gov."

Sharpie sucked in her breath and held it. Someone using that address had bought almost all of the technical documents she'd scanned in the past year.

"That's an ingenious little robot you have there," Danita said. "Where did you get it?"

Sharpie laid a possessive hand on Kitty. "I made it. Sorta."

"It looks like a scanner combined with a kid's helper-bot and a bin to hold the paper. Is that the only changes you made?"

Sharpie had to decide. Run or talk. The woman hadn't tried to come closer, so she decided to not press her luck. "I wrote some code to integrate them. I also upgraded the power supply and replaced the rubber tractor feed with an air blower to handle the paper without tearing it to hell."

The woman raised her eyebrows.

"How'd you find me?"

Danita smiled and nodded toward Kitty. "That robot has a transmitter that links into the local grid. Like a cell phone. You've been using it to send your files to the marketplace. We know how to track those signals."

Sharpie edged further along the wall, trying to get past the table so she'd have a clear path.

"Have you ever heard of the Frontier One orbital habitat?" Danita said.

Sharpie snorted. "Yeah. Are you trying to tell me you're from there?"

Danita nodded.

It sounded like total bullshit, but Sharpie so wanted it to be true. She'd always wondered if the tales about that wonderful castle in space were even true. "Was that your white plane that passed overhead?"

The woman nodded. "A shuttle. It can fly into space too. Look, we know you're an orphan, Sharpie. How old are you?"

She swallowed and looked down at the floor. "I don't know."

"We're working very hard up there to try and put all of this back together again," she said and gestured around the factory. "But we need people like you before we can do that."

"Is that why you're buying my manuals?"

"We don't really need the manuals. We kept buying them just long enough to find you."

That made her uneasy. Why would they do that?

"I have other things I can sell," Sharpie said.

"We don't need anything you have to sell. We need you."

"So you *are* a slaver?"

Danita had a strange look on her face, and tears welled in her eyes, then she shook her head. "No slavers up there. But we will give you a job and let you earn your keep."

"I don't get it," Sharpie said.

The woman wiped her eyes. "You saw things in this factory that might be valuable—like technical manuals—even after the gangs looted it?"

Sharpie nodded.

"It's kind of like that."

Sharpie still didn't get it, but she was starting to believe and trust the woman.

"Do you have food?"

"Yes, everyone eats up there."

"Can I take Kitty?" Sharpie said and laid a hand on the robot.

"No. We have weight limits on the shuttle, but you can make another one later if you like."

Sharpie realized she still held the marker and slipped it into her pocket. She would keep it if she could, but would be willing to sell it if things didn't work out.

-END-

William Ledbetter is a writer with more than forty speculative fiction stories and non-fiction articles published in markets such as Fantasy & Science Fiction, Jim Baen's Universe, Writers of the Future, Escape Pod, Daily Science Fiction, the SFWA blog, Yard Dog Press and Ad Astra. He's been a space and technology geek since childhood and spent most of his non-writing career in the aerospace and defense industry. He administers the Jim Baen Memorial Short Story Award contest for Baen Books and the National Space Society, is a member of SFWA, is the Science Track coordinator for the Fencon convention and is a consulting editor at Heroic Fantasy Quarterly. He lives near Dallas with his family and too many animals.

High Noon Zombies
John Moore

Navajo Joe was doing the Ghost Dance, as he did every Saturday, and Sam was beating time for him, as he did most Saturdays when he wasn't busy upholding the law. He watched Joe do the same dance over and over again, except each time with a slightly different variation, trying to find a dance that worked. After Joe danced each change he would make notes in a copy-book. The copy book was yellow with age.

When the sun was high enough that shade had all but disappeared, Sam stopped the tom-tom. "Getting pretty hot now, Joe," he called out. "Guess we better get on back to town."

Joe stopped dancing, took a drink from a tin can, and passed the can to Sam. "Your drumming's not so good today. Sam. Your heart isn't in it. You're brooding."

"I'm not brooding. I'm thinking."

"Brooding," said Joe. "What happened? The schoolteacher broke up with you again?"

"No. I mean, yes. She did, but that's not what I was thinking about. I was thinking that my life is going nowhere. My future has no future."

"You always get like this after a fight with Hazel. Anyway, your future is about to change."

"It is?"

"Everyone's life will change. The Ghost Dance, Sam. I can feel it. The next set of dances will be the breakthrough."

"Oh, right."

"Our warriors will rise from the dead and wage battle to reclaim our lands. The White Man's bullets..."

"The white man's bullets will be stopped and we will be driven back across the sea," said Sam. "Joe, how long have you been working on this dance?"

They mounted their horses. "Ten years. But it will all be worth it when I succeed. The red man will exterminate the white man once and for all."

"Uh huh."

Joe leaned from his saddle and slapped Sam on the back. "Don't worry, Sam. You will be spared. Everyone knows you are a friend of the red man. I'm sure we'll even get a job for you. Maybe sweeping up or something."

"Something to look forward to." They rode slowly back to Salt Flat, where Sam looked around with resignation, thinking he'd been here far too long.

Today, there was trouble, apparently. Salt Flat's three councilmen—Joe-Bob, Jim-Bob, and Bob—were waiting in front of the sheriff's office, looking very worried. Jim-Bob didn't even wait for Sam to dismount. "Sam, we just got word. Case Harden is on his way here. He's coming to kill you, Sam."

Sam and Joe exchanged glances. "Case Harden is dead, Jim-Bob. Been dead for six years."

"He rose from the dead," said Joe-Bob. "All three of them. Case Harden, Half-breed Birke, and Chinese Charlie. A whole buncha people were there for a funeral. They saw those sidewinders climbing out of their graves. They're coming on the train at high noon."

Sam nodded thoughtfully. He tied up his horse and put his hand on the door of the sheriff's office. "Then if you'll excuse me, there's something I've got to do."

The three councilmen look relieved. "You're going to meet the train, Sam?"

"Hell, no!" snapped Sam. "You think I'm crazy? I'm riding out of town."

Joe-Bob grabbed his arm. "Sam, you can't run out on us. You're the sheriff!"

"Hmm. You're right. As your sheriff, I do have a responsibility to this town." Sam unclipped his badge and pressed it into Joe-Bob's hand. "I resign. Well, that takes care of that. Adios."

"Sheriff!" Mickey, the telegraph operator, ran across the street, waving a telegraph slip. "Sheriff, Case Harden and his gang got off the train at Spittoon. They molested all the women. They killed at the men. And goats. But Case sent you a telegram first, Sheriff. He says he's coming to kill you."

"There, you see, Sam," said Jim-Bob. "We can't defend ourselves without you. It will be mass murder, just like Spittoon."

"There's only eight people in Spittoon."

"One, now," said Mickey. He ran back to the telegraph

office.

"Listen, Sam," said Bob. "We need you. We're desperate. And you won't be facing him alone. We'll be right behind you, just like last time."

"You ran away last time."

"Yes, but we ran away *behind* you. We didn't run away in front of you."

"Because we didn't want to spoil your aim," Joe-Bob added.

"I didn't know they had a woman in Spittoon," said Navajo Joe thoughtfully.

Joe-Bob turned on him. "Navajo Joe! This is your fault, damn it! You and your damn ghost dance. It finally worked. You brought dead warriors back to life."

"We were out by the old Indian graveyard," Sam pointed out. "If there were any dead Indians coming back to life, I'd have noticed them."

"Right," said Navajo Joe. "I mean—wait a minute—um."

"What?" said Sam.

"You were playing the tom-tom for me, Sam. Maybe that's it. That's got to be it. You were watching the dance and you're a white man, so it brought *your* enemies back to life."

"Send a telegram to Fort McKenzie," said Sam. "Call out the cavalry."

Mickey ran back out, waving another telegram. "Sheriff, Case and his men got off the train at Lockjaw. This time they killed all the women and molested all the men. And the chickens."

"I'll send a telegram," said Sam. "To all of you. Telling you where to forward my stuff. Goodbye."

Joe-Bob blocked the door. "Sam, you're panicking. What's the problem? You got them all last time."

"I was younger then. I was faster. And I barely escaped with my life. The odds of winning a gunfight like that a second time aren't real good."

He shouldered past the councilmen and into his office. Navajo Joe followed him inside. "Joe, you better start figuring out a way to reverse that ghost dance. Do the steps backward, or something."

Before Joe could reply, the door was flung open by a slim young woman with blue eyes and wheat-colored hair. "Sam!" She flung herself into the sheriff's arms. "Sam, what are you going to do?"

"Me? Hazel, I'm not doing anything. Except leaving town before those desperados kill me."

"But what about the rest of us, Sam? What about me? Sam, after all we've been meant to each other..."

"All we meant to each other ended last night when you dumped me."

"Dumped you?" Hazel looked baffled. "But I didn't——oh, Sam, you didn't think we were finished, did you? Just because we had a quarrel? A little tiff? A teensy weensy lovers' spat?"

"You called me a loser. You said I was the tin-plate sheriff of a two-bit town who would never amount to anything."

"But I meant it in a *good* way," Hazel wailed. "Sam, you can't go. There are goats and chickens depending on you."

"Hazel's right," said Joe. "You can't just pack up and leave now."

"Who said anything about packing? I'm just leaving."

"I mean Joe-Bob and Jim-Bob just rode off on our horses." He was looking out the window. "And Bob's running for the livery stable. Nope, he's too late. It looks like the rest of the town got every last horse and cleared out already. Here's Mickey again."

The telegraph operator ran across the street once more. He stopped in the doorway to catch his breath, then panted, "Sam, it turns out Fort McKenzie had been alerted already. A troop of calvary rode out and caught up with Case and his men at Snuffbox. It's all over, Sam."

"There, see," Sam told Hazel and Joe. "What did I tell you?"

"Case killed them all," said Mickey.

"Damn it.

"Killed their horses, too."

"Enough!"

"And he's coming to...."

"Yes, yes, I get it already!" Sam looked out the window, where the clock over Bob's barber shop showed both hands nearly at twelve. He pried Hazel's arms from around his neck and shoved her and Joe out the door. He strapped on a double action Colt, tucked a Starr carbine under his arm and stepped out into the street.

It was empty, except for Hazel and Joe. They were staring at the train. A gust of wind blew the smoke from the steam engine around the passenger car. Then out of the smoke stepped a tall man with a faded, gray army cap pulled low over his brow. Around his waist was strapped a gun belt, and oddly, a scabbard. Hair like moldy hay hung from under the hat, framing a scarred face whose skin hung in loose shreds. His eyes were sunk deep in his skull but they glittered with evil, and he carried with him a stench of death and decay. "Oh my Lord," said Hazel. "That's what a walking corpse looks like. Oh Sam, he's horrible."

"Who, Case?" Sam looked him over. "Nah, he always kind of looked like that." Behind Case, a tall, blond man with blue eyes, pale skin, and a broad brimmed black Stetson got off the train. "And that's Half-breed Birke."

"Half-breed?" said Joe. "That's the whitest white man I ever saw."

"Half Swedish, half Norwegian. Very touchy about the Norwegian part."

"Well, who wouldn't be?"

"He's very fast. Very dangerous. And kind of depressed."

The last man to get off the train was shorter, with black hair and a long, drooping black mustache. "Chinese Charlie," explained Sam. "The most sadistic killer in the history of Yokahama."

"Yokahama is in Japan, Sam," said Hazel.

"I know. But nickname committee said that Japanese Charlie didn't have the same ring."

The three men squinted in the harsh sunlight, then began a slow, steady march toward Sam. Hazel clutched Sam's arm. "I've changed my mind, Sam. You should leave town after all."

"A little late now, Hazel," He shoved her toward the barber shop. "Get inside somewhere. Joe, see if you can do something with that dance."

Half a block away, the three desperados halted, resting their hands on the butt of their guns. Sam kept his voice as casual as he could. "That's far enough, Case. You know the speech I'm about to make. So there's no need for me to actually make it."

Case grinned, showing a mouthful of rotting gums and loose yellow teeth. "That's the one where you promise that if we throw down our guns and come quietly, you'll see we get a fair trial?"

"Yep, that's it."

"Has that ever worked?"

"Dunno'. I got it out of a dime novel."

"I ain't much of a literary man, Sam."

They were momentarily distracted when the door of the barbershop opened and Bob dragged Hazel inside. Apparently figuring this was not the time to make new enemies, she popped her head back out long enough to say, "Afternoon, Mr. Harden. Lovely day, is it not?" before slamming the door closed again.

Case turned his attention back to Sam. "Make your move, Sheriff."

Later, the few bystanders who stuck around to watch the fight agreed that if he had slowed down any in six years, it wasn't by much. In an instant the Colt was in his hand, and the hammer made three rapid clicks.

Sam said, "What the hell?"

Case, Half-breed Birke, and Chinese Charlie were smiling. Their hands still rested on their gun butts. They hadn't even tried to draw.

Sam raised his carbine. It likewise refused to fire. He dropped it in the dust. His three antagonists were laughing out loud now. "It's that old Navajo Ghost Dance, Sam," Case called out. "It really does stop the white man's bullets. Navajo Joe finally did it."

And then all three drew their real weapons.

Sam turned and ran.

His boarding house was two blocks away and deserted. He raced up the stairs to his room. A large trunk sat at the foot of his bed. He got it open, pulled out his old uniform, and tossed it aside. Underneath was his cavalry saber. He carried it back down the stairs and almost ran into Chinese Charlie.

Sam was long out of practice with a military saber. But Chinese Charlie was not only out of practice, he was dead. To parry with a samurai sword requires a great deal of speed, speed that Charlie no longer had. Sam disabled his sword arm with a thrust to the shoulder. Charlie dropped his katana, and then Sam cut his head off.

It was the traditional method of killing the undead and it seemed to work. But his respite was short. Half-breed Birke was at the door. He was carrying a Viking sword.

"Where in the hell did they find these swords?" Sam wondered. But he didn't time to reflect on the matter. Birke did not seem the least bit out of practice, and he wasn't letting mere death slow him down. The Half-Breed swung his sword fast and hard, the blows nearly knocking Sam's saber from his hands. Sam had no chance to attack, it was all he could do to parry the blows. Behind him the hall led to the boardinghouse kitchen. Sam gave up the fight and ran into it.

He dove over the kitchen table, then shoved it into the hallway. It only stopped Birke for a moment. He cleaved it in two with his broadsword, strode between the pieces and a raised his sword for a killing thrust. But a moment was all Sam had needed. His hand came out from a cupboard holding a glass jar. "Back off, Birke. Or I smash this jar of lingonberry preserves."

It stopped Birke cold. His eyes locked on the jar of ruby red berries. "You're bluffing, Sam."

"Yeah? Try me. This came all the way from Chicago. There ain't another jar in the territories."

Birke licked his cracked lips. "I haven't tasted *lingonsylt* in six years."

"Aww. Then have some now." Sam flung the jar at Birke's face. The Half-breed instinctively raised his hands to catch it, and that gave Sam the opening he needed to drive his sword in deep. Birke fell to his knees. The jar hit the floor in front of him and smashed. He stared at it in disgust. "Cranberries!" Then his head hit the floor with them.

And immediately Sam was attacked by Case Harden. The ghost dance outlaw was wielding a cavalry saber, and he was damn good with it. It was all Sam could do to parry his thrusts. Case kept his hideous grin as he drove Sam out the back door of the boardinghouse. "Hell, Sam. I should have tried this trick six years ago."

Sam was short of breath. "You mean let your cronies wear me out first so you can move in for the kill?"

"That's right." Case got under Sam's guard and slashed his chest. Blood flowed from the cut. "My company used the same trick against the Cheyenne." Another vicious slash across Sam's arm caused him to drop his sword. "It worked then, too." He feinted towards Sam's face. Sam stumbled backwards and fell. Before he could rise, Case had the point of his sword against Sam's throat. "Any last words, Sheriff?"

At which point Case Harden's head exploded.

"Um, not really," said Sam. He stood up and brushed scoops of desiccated flesh off his vest. He was looking over the corpse when Hazel came across the yard. She was holding Sam's carbine.

"Hazel? How did you do that?"

"White man's bullets," explained Hazel. She worked the lever on the carbine, ejecting the spent shell. "Navajo Joe said the Ghost Dance stops the white *man's* bullets. He didn't say anything about the white *woman's* bullets."

"Trust a schoolteacher to come up with something like that."

Hazel took off her scarf and wrapped it around Sam's arm. "You know what this could mean, Sam? Firepower translates into political power. If only women can use guns, a lot of things could change in this country."

"Like what?"

"We could institute a program of national health care."

Navajo Joe reached the boarding house in time to see them walk off, arm in arm. "Who's going to pay for it?" Sam was saying.

Joe smiled and began to make plans for the following Saturday. The high noon zombies showed he was on the right track to creating a working ghost dance. He just needed to fine tune it a bit.

John Moore is an engineer who lives and works in Houston, Texas. He is the author of two dozen professionally-published short stories and six novels in the science fiction and fantasy genre. His latest novel, *The Lightning Horse*, is available from Yard Dog Press.

Moore can be reached through his website at <www.sff.net/people/John.Moore>.

Roll for Initiative

Tracy S. Morris

Figarella burst through the door and paused, marionette-loose limbs askew and parchment falling from her scroll bag like dead leaves. She looked around with wild, bloodshot eyes, sniffled once, then pushed between Zook and Lula in a beeline for the cauldron in the corner, dropping dice along the way.

Zook closed her milk-white eyes and turned an ear toward the noise. "Was that your cousin, Figgy?" She asked Lula.

Rather than answer, Lula picked her way across the die-strewn floor. It wouldn't do to impale her foot on one of the pyramid-shaped ones, or fall into the fire because she tripped on the rug, or Roger the rat-dog sleeping on the rug, or her own feet...again.

"Figgy?" Lula reached for the girl, but pulled back as Figarella stuffed roll after roll of parchment into the cauldron. She licked her lips and tried again. "Aren't those the scrolls for your turn-based encounter simulation... thingy?"

"I hate barbarian training school!" Figarella snapped. "They never do any real barbarianing. It's all this ink-and-parchment tabletop crap. When do I get to see a *real* encounter?"

Lula looked down at Roger and shrugged. *Teens. Can't live with them, can't catapult them to Cathay.*

In part, Lula sympathized. When she was a barbarian pup, all the little barbabies got hands-on training. That was where she lost her first two fingers, brained her brother, shot her teacher in the backside and learned all the words to *How Many Drunken Vikings Does it Take to Burn Old Agincourt Down?* In retrospect, she really should've quit the family business sooner.

"There aren't any real encounters." Lula reminded her cousin gently. "We're civilized barbarians now."

"Did something happen in school today?" Zook asked.

Lula cast a sidelong glance at her partner. The thought hadn't even occurred to her, but it made sense. Though sightless, Zook sure saw a lot.

"They killed Ka-Thun-Ka!" Figgy wailed, then threw the

last of her dice into the cauldron after the scrolls.

"Ka-Thun-Ka?" Zook cocked her head to the side.

Lula scratched behind her ear in thought. "Must be her combat avatar." She looked to Roger again as if he had all the answers, but the little dog merely licked himself in a rather private place.

"Lord Ka-Thun-Ka. The bold slayer of the seven-headed dragon. Master of the Way of Wong. He who wished nothing more than to crush his enemies, drive them forth, and hear the lamination of their women."

"Isn't that supposed to be lamentation?" Zook asked from behind her hand.

"She actually does mean lamination," Lula replied. "It's a new form of preservation."

"And now he's dead!" Figgy carried on as if she couldn't hear them.

Lula put a consoling hand on her cousin's shoulder. "He's just someone you invented for training scenarios, isn't he? How can you kill a fictional character?"

"He was me!" She turned into Lula's shoulder and sobbed into her chain mail. "I lived his adventures! His glory was my glory! They killed a little bit of me when they killed him!"

Lula stared in horror at the salty tears wreaking who knows what kind of havoc on her armor. She patted Figgy's shoulder and tried not to think of the hours of cleaning and oiling ahead of her.

Roger's bark drew Lula's attention. The pup barked at the fire, which crackled, popped and burned vibrant purple flames. On instinct, she grasped his collar and hurled him into Zook's arms. She caught the pup with a grunt.

"What—" Before Zook could finish her confused question, Lula grasped her wrist, and pulled her and Figgy from the room. Seconds later, the cauldron split apart in a blinding flash of light.

"Is everyone okay?" Lula asked as she opened the door to let out the smoke.

"I am," a very masculine voice answered from somewhere in the obscuring smoke.

Lula fumbled for her mace, only to grab the wrong end. She attempted to flip it over, only to drop the smooth, round head onto the remaining three toes on her right foot. She fell to the floor, writhing, clutching her foot and biting back words she didn't want her cousin to know she knew.

Figgy stepped between Lula and the dissipating smoke, sword drawn to defend them against the unseen menace. "You could call it a tottering, rude-growing bugbear," she offered helpfully.

"Where did you learn those words?" Lula sat up, massaging her foot and keeping one eye on the dissipating smoke.

"English class." She rolled her eyes. "If we're going to invade, the professors want us to know what we're being called."

The smoke cleared, revealing a tall, muscular man dressed in little more than a pair of fur shorts and a bandolier.

The point of Figgy's sword lowered. "Ka-Thun-Ka?" she said in astonishment.

"That's your avatar?" Lula's brain bypassed the instinct to wonder where he came from, and plugged straight into her libido. "Hello, Doctor! Aren't you a natural twenty!"

Ka-Thun-Ka looked confused; it seemed to be his default expression. "Is this Heaven?"

"Would you like it to be?" Lula asked as she stood.

Figgy punched her shoulder. "He's my avatar. I invented him. Technically, that's my son!"

"Oh, ick!" Zook shuddered.

"Where have those genes been hiding?" Lula sighed. To Ka-Thun-Ka, she said, "No, this isn't Heaven."

"Then I went to the other place." He frowned. "That explains your face."

Lula growled. "No inheritance for you!"

"How did you get here?" Figgy asked the question that Lula hadn't. She took Ka-Thun-Ka's hand and patted it reassuringly. "What's the last thing you remember?"

He squinted, temporarily rendering his vacant features into something that resembled a constipated squirrel. "I was in the mines of marshmallow and... the rocks fell?"

Figgy nodded to corroborate his story. "That's how my B.M. killed him. Rocks fall, everyone dies."

"B.M.?" Zook asked.

"Barbarian Master." Lula said. "The one who runs the encounter—usually whichever grad student is sucking up to the dean."

"That still doesn't explain how he got here," Zook said.

Lula's gaze fell to the scorched bone dice and bits of parchment on the floor. "One of those scrolls must have had a summoning spell on it. Burning it with the others could have pulled Ka-Thun-Ka into our world."

"How do you know that?" Figgy asked.

"Zook and I deliver messages for the king." Lula said. "We've been sent out with a missive that way more than once."

"One of the other students must have made the spell," Zook said. "I bet your B.M. can help find out who. Then we can make them reconstruct the spell, and send your avatar back where he belongs."

Both Figgy and Ka-Thun-Ka looked unhappy about that.

"Back?" he asked.

"Not into the mines," Figgy said.

Lula patted Ka-Thun-Ka's muscular, manly bicep—to reassure him, not to enjoy the feel of smooth muscle under supple skin. "I'm sure we can find another encounter to drop him into."

"Thank you, ma'am... You can stop now." Ka-Thunk-Ka fled to the window and pulled down the curtains in an attempt to fashion a more modest toga. The effort was practically wasted, since the fabric was translucent.

"Before we send him back, we should get him some chain mail like the rest of the family wears," Figgy said. "That fur getup isn't very protective."

Lula sighed. "Seems a shame to cover up what his maker gave him."

"I'm his maker," Figgy said, covering Lula's eyes.

Lula batted away her hands. "If you didn't want me looking, why did you make him..." She looked him up and down. "Slab-like?"

Figarella held her arms up and shrugged. "I don't remember doing that. Maybe it came with the high strength score?"

"Maybe if you hadn't burned your scrolls, we could look it up," Zook put in.

"We wouldn't be in this mess if she hadn't burned her scrolls," Lula reminded Zook. Across the room, Ka-Thun-Ka turned to look out the window. The toga outlined his shapely fur-covered backside. "Not that I'm complaining," Lula added.

Figgy led them to a tavern called *Dante's Kitchen.* There, at the back of the room, her B.M. sat on a throne of skulls with harem girls wearing gauze as sheer as Ka-Thun-Ka's toga posed at each elbow. His dark hair fell in long waves over his mail-clad shoulders, though he kept his mustache trimmed neat and close around his face.

"Your B.M. is a traditionalist, I see," Lula noted.

Figgy crossed her arms and nodded. "With a weakness for sorority girls."

Just then, the B.M.'s gaze fell on them. He yelped, dropped his goblet of mead mid-quaff, and hid behind the harem girl on the right.

"Hey!" the harem girl snapped at him, shaking off his grip. She turned and pushed her index finger into his chest. "You aren't giving me enough extra credit to be your meat-shield." With that, she and the other harem girl fled the room. He dove behind the throne of skulls, pulling all of his limbs tight to present less of a target.

"And here I thought this would be a challenge." Lula cracked her knuckles and grinned.

"Are you sure it's us he's expecting?" Zook asked. "People don't normally make the quaking in mortal terror sounds when we approach."

Lula sighed. "I hate it when you talk sense."

"Maybe he's in awe of my presence?" Ka-Thun-Ka guessed.

"Who wouldn't be?" Lula said. "But somehow, I don't think that's it."

Heedless of their side conversation, Figgy stalked up to the throne and shouted over it at her B.M. "Gordy! Come out and face us!"

"What are you doing here? I flunked you right out of class!" Gordy's nasally, whining voice, and little else, came from behind the throne.

"I need your help!" Figgy said.

"Go away!" Aa single hand raised in a shooing motion.

"Why, you spineless coward!" Figgy put her hand so her hips. While she yelled at the cowering B.M., Roger crawled from Zook's arms and sniffed at the macabre furniture. He barked once, then seized a jawbone and began to gnaw.

"What is it boy?" Zook placed a hand on the throne. "Why is this so knobb—ugh!" She wiped her hand on her tunic. "I touched dead humans! Lula, you could've warned me! "

"Sorry, little distracted here." Lula's gaze zinged from a yelling Figgy to the hiding Gordy to Zook like a shuttlecock in play. "Do you think the kitchen serves popcorn? This is better than theatre!"

"Why is this even in a tavern?" Zook muttered. "It must violate some law the king has about good taste." Just then her questing fingers fell on a pile of parchment. "I can read this!" She vibrated in excitement. "Whoever wrote it pressed so hard, it left an imprint on the page."

Lula moved to look over Zook's shoulders. "There's no ink," she said. "It must be an imprint of the page above it. What does it say?"

"According to this, Gordy killed Ka-Thun-Ka and flunked Figgy on purpose by fudging his dice rolls."

A hurt look crossed Figgy's face. "What? Why?"

"So that you wouldn't be around when he introduced his own player: Tunk-Ra, Queen of Barbarians." Zook reported as her questing fingers traced down the lines of the parchment. "She's just a female version of Lord Ka-Thun-Ka."

"You stole my homework!" Figgy hissed at Gordy. The steel of her sword rang as she pulled it from her scabbard.

Gordy backed away from his throne, cackling in a worrisome, evil-sorcerer way that usually led to people being turned into frogs or banjoes or frogs with banjoes.

"Take your homework? I improved on it! Behold!" He held aloft what Lula thought must be the cover-sheet to the blank page that Zook was reading. Then he threw it into a cauldron over the fire.

Remembering how Ka-Thun-Ka came into their world, Lula overturned a trestle table and pulled Zook and Roger behind it for safety. Figgy and Ka-Thun-Ka followed seconds before Gordy's cauldron exploded.

When the smoke finally cleared, Lula peeked up over the table to see that a female verson of Ka-Thun-Ka stood before them— complete with a fur bikini.

Gordy pointed at them, practically foaming at the mouth. "They know enough to get me expelled! Get them!"

"I'll handle this!" Ka-Thun-Ka vaulted the table and faced off against Thunk-Ra. "I warn you"—he shook a finger at Thunk-Ra—"I know Wong Way and I'm not afraid to use it."

"Wong Way? Ha!" Thunk-Ra tossed her head and laughed. "Your Wong Way is nothing against a master of Wok-Dish-Way!"

"You challenge me?" Ka-Thunk-Ka bared his teeth in a feral grin. "Then let us battle in the arena of the Chef of Iron, and we will see who is master. Name your weapon!"

"I choose Sow-Ah-Do!" Thunk-Ra said.

"A tough skill to master." Ka-Thunk-Ra nodded in approval. "Very well, To the kitchen! And may the best chef win!"

"I shall!" she replied.

As the two warriors strode into the kitchen, Lula whispered in Zook's ear. "May I borrow your seeing eye dog? I need to send a message."

"To whom?" Zook asked.

"The inn up the street," Lula said. "This battle is going to take a while, so I'm ordering our lunch elsewhere." She scrawled a note across a scrap of parchment with a chunk of charcoal, and then tied the note to Roger's collar. With a wink, she sent him on his way.

Just as Roger returned, Gordy stood and banged his barbarian mace on the floor. "Time's up! Bring out your dishes!" The Thunk twins— as Lula now thought of them— emerged from the kitchen, each carrying a covered dish.

"Something's been bothering me," Lula whispered to Figgy. "Why does your barbarian avatar cook?"

"It's a quirk of the Gordy edition rules," Figgy said. "If you give your player an odd attribute, you can put extra points into your combat skills."

"Gordy came up with that idea, huh?" Lula cocked her head. "What did his last avatar look like?"

"Pretty much a sentient rock. But if his teammates loaded him into a catapult, it annihilated the other side."

Both Ka-Thun-Ka and Thunk-Ra lifted the covers from their dishes, revealing their work. Ka-Thun-Ka carried a plate of cinnamon rolls, while Thunk-Ra's plate held a batard of bread. They placed their serving dishes on a trestle table to await judgment.

"I'll judge this contest," Gordy said.

"That's not fair!" Figgy protested. "You can't judge a contest involving your own avatar."

Gordy glared at her. "Fine!" He pointed at Zook. "Let her judge. We'll make it a blind taste test." His annoying, nasal laugh was the only one in the room.

Lula gripped her mace. "You seem to have a breathing problem there, Gordo. I can fix that for you."

"It's fine, Lula," Zook said to calm her down. "Let's just get this over with."

Figgy led Zook to the table, and placed a roll in her hand. Lula held her breath as Zook took a bite. She worked her jaw like a cow chewing cud, then she swallowed in an exaggerated motion. With a gasp, she smacked her lips. "Can I get some water?"

"It's bad!" Gordy jeered.

"It's a little dense," Zook hedged.

"A little!" Gordy brayed like a donkey. "Were you trying to make Rock N' Rolls? Your rolls are so dense, they had to repeat first grade! Did you drop them and pick up stones by mistake? Hadrian called! He wants his wall back!"

"My Do is only So-So." Ka-Thun-Ka lowered his head. "I am ashamed."

"You haven't won yet!" Figgy said to Thunk-Ra. "Zook still has to try the bread!"

They all lapsed into silence as Zook tore a hunk off of the bread. She turned it around in her meaty paws. "Do I have to?" she whined. "It already feels rock-hard."

Ka-Thun-Ka and Thunk-Ra put their heads together to confer. "The Do didn't rise," Ka-Thun-Ka said loudly enough for everyone to hear.

"Maybe we should have selected Coo-Kee-Do." Thunk-Ra shrugged.

"If the judge won't arbitrate, then I win by default!" Gordy crowed.

Figgy snatched up one of Ka-Thun-Ka's rock-hard rolls. "Hey, Gordy! Arbitrate this!" She flung the food at his head. Gordy ducked and snatched up Thunk-Ra's batard of bread.

"Batter up!" He giggled as he swung the bread like a club. The roll met the batard with a crack. All eyes except Zook's followed its trajectory as it flew out the front entrance between the swinging doors.

"Ow!" A tall, blonde man in well-buffed plate armor walked through the door, holding the roll in one hand. The other hand, he held firmly over his left eye.

"Dean Ex Machina!" Figgy and Gordy gasped.

Gordy tried to hide the bread club behind his back. "This isn't what it looks like!" he said.

The dean's eye narrowed. "It looks like a bake-off."

"This is exactly what it looks like." Gordy dropped the batard and kicked it under the table.

"Save it, Gordy. I know what you've done." The dean pulled

a scrap of parchment from his breastplate. "Who owns the dog that carried this?"

"We do," Zook and Lula said.

The dean took a hasty step away from Lula, covering his backside. "You were one of my students, and you you shot me. I might have guessed that you would be mixed up in this." He fixed his glare back on Gordy. "I'm throwing you out of barbarian school for cheating. And I'm letting Figarella back in."

"But... But..." Gordy dropped to his knees and wrapped his arms around the dean's knees, blubbering into his shiny armor.

"What about the Thunk Twins?" Lula asked.

"What do I look like? Your own personal problem-solver? Figure it out yourself!" He kicked Gordy away. "Now I've got to go polish this before the knees rust, and slap a steak over my eye." Muttering in disgust, he stalked from the room.

"Now what?" Figgy threw her hands up. "We're worse off than before, because now we've got two avatars!"

Lula looked from Zook to the blank pages. "Maybe we can trace out the imprint of the spell?"

"That could work," Zook said as she slid her hand over the page again.

The Thunk twins put their heads together for another conference. "Actually," Ka-Thun-Ka said. "We'd like to stay here."

Thunk-Ra nodded along. "We're going to open a restaurant. And if that doesn't work, I think we can do something with that bat and roll idea. Maybe a game?"

"What?" Figgy worked her jaw, eyes bulged. "Well, if you won't go back, can I go instead?"

Lula gripped Figgy's shoulders and looked hard into her face. "Are you sure?"

Figgy nodded. "I told you that I'm tired of this theoretical crap. I want to do some real barbarianing."

"Okay." Lula pulled her into a hug, then handed her the batard. "Then take this. And make me proud."

Figgy beamed in happiness.

While Lula inked the parchment along the depressions, Ka-Thun-Ka helped Figgy find one of Gordy's spare manuals. Then Lula handed the scroll to Figgy.

"Tell the other barbarians goodbye for me," Figgy said. She threw the parchment into the Kitchen's cauldron, and vanished.

"Think she'll be okay?" Zook asked.

"I'm sure she will," Lula said as she watched the Thunk twins clear away dice and rock-hard buns. "It helps that she knows her roll in life."

Tracy S. Morris is the kind of person who would like to get up to shenanigans, but more frequently has misadventures (don't ask her about the exploding pants).

When Tracy isn't involved in the occasional tabletop RPG or watching old episodes of Iron Chef and Hell's Kitchen, she takes care of her husband and two kids (which mainly involves making sure they don't walk out the door with their underpants on their heads).

Tracy is the author of three books through Yard Dog Press: *Tranquility*, *Bride of Tranquility*, and *Medieval Misfits: Renaissance Rejects*. *Medieval Misfits* contains the further adventures of Zook, Lula and Roger.

You can find Tracy on the web at tracysmorris.com.

Bloodsucking Monkeys
Ethan Nahté

Marima and Aroka were hunched over their kill, the *yaguara* that had been attacking their dwindling tribe along the *Igarapé do Mucuim*, the river that snaked its way through the heart of the Amazon Jungle, deep within the southern Amazon Basin. The animal was "the beast who killed its prey in one bound."

The boys, both in their teens, were preparing the spotted predator before tying it to a nearby piece of mahogany to transport back to their village. They were of the Juma tribe, the "fierce" people, numbering less than one hundred in the mid-twentieth century.

Aroka extracted his sharpened stone knife from its tapir-skin sheath. He grasped the strong upper jaw and forced the head back, causing the tongue to roll out to the side. He drew the knife edge across the white fur beneath to slit the big cat's throat, the warm blood spurting out across his hands.

Marima was squatted near the black and yellow tail of the *yaguara,* stripping vines from a nearby tree. He asked, "Do you know the story of the bloodsucking monkeys?"

Aroka looked up and shook his head. Although the old men told stories around the nightly fires, sometimes a story would only be told within a hut and not shared with the entire tribe for many generations, risking becoming lost to time, like the Juma themselves.

Aroka was the last male in his hut. His father died from disease after contact with explorers. It was the last time his tribe had seen white men before the natives disappeared even deeper into the forest. That was years ago when Aroka was the size of a spider monkey.

His grandfather had died a couple of years later while hunting *caitetu munde*, the giant peccary. He killed the peccary, but not before he slipped in the mud while throwing his spear. The angered hog, a spear protruding from its ribs and stuck deep into its heart, repeatedly gored his grandfather before the beast succumbed. The meat was cooked at the funeral feast in honor of his grandfather.

Marima continued weaving his tale as he lashed the flexible vines and reeds about a broken mahogany branch just long enough to transport their kill. "My father tells me this story comes down to him from many grandfathers back. He says that before white explorers crossed the great water and invaded our lands, taking our gold, rubber, cashews and parrots, all the people of the Amazon feared a certain breed of monkey."

"Which monkey?" Aroka asked.

"That has been forgotten, for the monkey no longer exists. It would attack people, landing upon its victim and sinking its sharp teeth deep within their throat. It killed the person but never ate them. Instead, it only sucked their blood. Because people feared these monkeys, no one hunted them for food...only for defense.

"But when the Europeans arrived, wearing their metal clothing, they were safe from the monkeys' attacks. With their sticks of thunder they killed all the bloodsucking monkeys, but not before a monkey infected another."

Aroka's eyes widened in surprise as he watched his friend search the canopy of branches blocking out the afternoon sun. He asked, "Do you mean a person became so cursed?"

"No, because to become one of the accursed, a victim had to drink from the monkey after the monkey drank from the victim. No person ever drank."

"Then what creature would do such a horrible thing?" Aroka asked, impatient to learn more.

"One night while seeking a meal of insects, a bat, no larger than my thumb, stopped to rest upon a leaf high in a tree. The bat could sense something moving nearby. At the last moment the bat dropped from the leaf, just escaping the vicious strike of a young tree boa waiting patiently on the limb, hidden by the leaves. The bat fluttered down, banging his wing against a limb and landing in the branches of a smaller tree.

"The smaller tree was the resting place of a family of bloodsucking monkeys. The stunned bat had landed on the shoulder of one such monkey, startling it awake. The monkey snatched the bat and bit into its back. The bat, in pain and scared for its life, twisted around and bit the monkey on the tongue, drawing blood and drinking it down. The monkey howled and slung the little bat into the darkness where it bounced against another large leaf and slid down deep into a Parrot's Beak flower."

Aroka stopped wiping the blood from his blade on the claw-like orange petals of the same flower. He glanced inside the partially-opened bloom to see if it contained a bat.

Marima hadn't named that specific flower to scare his friend; it was the very flower his father had retold in his tale, but he found the irony to be quite funny. Stifling a laugh, Marima continued. "The bat, weak from its injuries, lay there all night, and for two more days and a night. On the third night the bat arose, hungry. It scrambled out of the flower and sougnt its prey, finding a large bug. But the bat discovered it wasn't hungry for the meat, it only wanted the blood. It drank but found that the bug's blood did not quench its thirst. The bat decided that bugs were not going to be large enough and it would take too many to drink its fill."

"So what did it do?" Aroka anxiously asked, enthralled by the tale of his friend. "Did the bat attack people?"

"No," Marima replied. "The bat first went after monkeys, learning to quietly sneak up on them by landing then hopping and crawling along a branch. Then the bat would make a small cut in an ankle or leg and lap up the blood. It didn't take much of the monkey's blood to fill him."

"Does this bloodsucking bat still live?"

"No," Marima said. "But the problem is that bats are very sociable and live very close together in their colonies. The blood curse spread quickly, infecting the other bats in that colony. Soon all of that particular type of bat became what is known as a vampire bat. My grandfather, listening to my father tell the family the horrible tale, said that from the brief time he spent around a white explorer he learned that there are only three species of vampire bats in the world, all here in South America."

Aroka stared at the blood on his hands. The spray from the cat's jugular vein had speckled his legs and feet with red, some of it still dripping. He quickly wiped at his legs and rubbed his hands on the fur of his kill. "So we are in danger?"

"No, Aroka. Once the white settlers brought over horses and cattle, the bats learned to feed quietly on these animals. It is rare that they bite a human. And they never take enough blood to kill. But my grandfather also said that most of the world is scared of bats, fearing that they will drink their blood or turn into a human-like creature and suck their blood. The bats are feared because they once protected themselves."

"That is crazy," Aroka expressed in disbelief.

"Yes, but the outsiders make stories of bats who attack for blood to scare people. The people of the rainforest know it is a myth. As long as we don't eat or harm the bats, we won't become cursed."

"I'm just glad there are no more bloodsucking monkeys," Aroka said.

Marima laughed while they began tying the legs of the *yaguara* to the staff. As they lifted the body he asked, "Have I told you about the Spirit Cat that haunts this jungle?"

Aroka shook his head before they moved forward; unaware of the lurking beast with reddish-yellow eyes watching intently, its sharp claws penetrating the thick tree limb where it silently hid above while the jungle floor darkened with sunset.

Ethan Nahté is an author, journalist, screenwriter, photographer and musician. He has also worked in TV/Film and Radio. He has nearly two-dozen stories and poems published in various anthologies and e-zines. His work spans horror, historical fiction, fantasy, sci-fi and young adult. He recently finished his first novel and will be releasing his first collection *Of Monsters & Madmen*, eight previously published stories along with two new stories, complete with art and introductions for each tale.

Destination: Uranus
Jody Lynn Nye

"Outhouse One, Outhouse One, do you copy?" Mariella McCarthy's voice echoed throughout the juddering, specially sealed cosmic four-holer hurtling through space.

Granny Geraldine McCarthy grabbed the heavy phone receiver off the wall and clapped it to her good ear. Her small, lined face wrinkled even more in irritation.

"Copy what? What am I supposed to be copying? I got enough to do steering this thing. We almost just hit Neptune!"

"I tole you she should'a gotten her eyes checked before taking off from Earth," a voice said in the background.

"You shut your mouth if you can't show respect, Brady Joe McCarthy," Granny snapped. "I might be eighty-six years old, but I can still bend you over my knee! And y'all call me Captain, you got that?"

"Yes'm," Brady said at once. Granny might have been well below bantam weight, but no one messed with her. "Sorry, ma'am."

"We're on course for Uranus," Lucy McCarthy said, from her seat next to Granny. Her headphones were almost buried in her cloud of kinky black hair. Her big brown eyes shone with excitement. "Should be about two hours now before we make orbit."

"Uranus. Heh heh heh," chortled Roger Zelby, his lower lip drooping with glee. "You said Uranus."

Granny and Lucy glared at the big, burly man, then looked at each other.

"Why'd we have to bring him?" Granny asked. "I told you we ought to leave the big dumb lump at home."

"We needed someone to wear the red shirt," Lucy said. "It's one of the rules of *Star Trek*. I explained that, Granny— I mean, Captain. If anyone attacks us, we hide behind him. If they eat him, they'll probably let us go."

Granny regarded her eldest granddaughter with pride. She had cheered when her son Zeke had married one of the Felton girls down the road; it had been the smartest thing her son had ever done. Lucy had been to junior college and majored in *math*. She knew stuff. Therefore, she'd been the only real choice in the holler to be the science officer on board Outhouse One.

"He sure will be no loss," Granny agreed. "Now, what is it you were callin' me about, Mariella? I got a ship to run."

"Just wanted to know how much of the moonshine you run through?" Mariella said.

"That ain't my concern! Mose McShea McCarthy, what's the gauge read?"

The engineering officer, a broad-bellied man in his fifties with receding brown hair running to gray huddled on the farthest seat, looked up from his copy of *Field and Stream* and leaned back to tap the glass bubble sticking out of the brass pipe in the back wall of the outhouse.

"Got two thirds of the tank left," Mose said. "This stuff's got a real kick!"

"Well, it's genuine moon-shine," Lucy replied, looking justifiably proud. "Mose and I brewed it out of that green cheese we took off the Moon last trip out."

"Moonshine made out of cheese. As if things don't smell bad enough in here," Granny said, wrinkling her nose. "I don't know what the folks on Uranus are gonna say."

"Heh heh heh. You said Uranus!"

Granny and Lucy exchanged another look.

"Sure we can't leave him there when we go home?" Granny asked.

"His mama might miss him," Lucy said.

"She needs to use a bigger shotgun, then."

The truck backup horn that they had mounted on the front of the outhouse started honking wildly. Lucy peered through the half-moon shaped window cut in the door. A blue sphere edged into the irregular field of view and started to get bigger and bigger. Lucy beamed.

"We're almost there!" she exclaimed, then gasped. "Hard right, Granny! There's a moon out there!"

Granny took hold of the 1956 Chevy steering wheel mounted in front of her seat and hauled it hard over. As she did, they all heard a tremendous bang. The outhouse shifted noticeably and let out a moaning creak that shook the walls. Lucy flinched. Hissing and whistling came from the rear of the outhouse.

"Godawmighty!" Mose said, looking up from his magazine, with a frown on his big, sun-reddened face. "It shouldn't be making sounds like that."

"Well, what do you think's wrong?" Granny asked.

"Dunno. Either she's about to calve, or..."

A horrendous shriek erupted, drowning him out. The craft began to shake even more than it had before.

"Or what?" Granny demanded, pitching her voice high over the noise.

"Or somethin' hit the fuel tank," Mose allowed.

"What's gonna hit us all the way out here?"

"Gotta be an asteroid," Lucy said. "We didn't hit the moon. It's still out there."

"Ass-teroid!" Roger chortled.

"Stop laughin', you fool!" Granny said, staring in horror out of the crescent-shaped window at the widening expanse of blue. "I think mebbe we're gonna crash. Grab hold of somethin' and start praying!"

Granny held tight to the wheel. The planet that they'd been aiming for ever since it heaved into view got bigger and bigger, until it filled the entire window. Lucy and the others clutched the wooden seats under their bottoms with both hands.

"We can't survive," Lucy said, her eyes wide with terror. "If we strike down hard, we're gonna leave a crater the size of Chattanooga!"

"Hang on," Granny yelled. "If we're gonna die, it'll be in the name of science!"

The ride was rougher than going down the Cumberland Gap on a flat tire. Granny gritted her teeth as they plunged down through thick, blue-white clouds. Just before the impact, she closed her eyes and made her peace with God.

Sploop!

The outhouse didn't so much bang into the surface as splash. Granny got her wits together faster than the others did. She sprang up and reached for the doorknob. Lucy grabbed her wrist.

"Don't do it," she said. "It could be below freezing out there!"

"I got my long johns on," Granny said. She beckoned. "If I'm still alive, I want to see what's out there. You come on with me, girl." She pointed a finger at the men. "You two lugs get off your bottoms and come along."

"Yes'm," Roger and Mose chorused. Mose gathered up his magazine and rolled it into a tin can nailed to the wall next to the hanging catalog that served as toilet paper and heaved himself up. Roger waved his arms and grunted, but he couldn't get up by himself. His big rear end was stuck in the hole from the impact. Lucy and Mose braced their feet on either side of him and took hold of his arms.

"Ready?" Lucy said, with a nod at Mose. "One, two, three!" They hauled hard.

Roger popped loose and hurtled past them right into the door. It opened, and he stumbled out into the light blue landscape.

"That boy just got the right instincts of a red shirt," Granny said approvingly. She and the others followed a little more cautiously. Mose shouldered a double-barreled shotgun. Granny knew Lucy was packing, but she was too much of a lady to let her personal weaponry show under her neat khaki trousers or her Hopkinsville Community College sweatshirt. It'd come out if it was needed. Same for herself. She had a fully loaded .38 revolver stuck down the outside of her right boot under her long denim skirt. Hostile aliens wouldn't know what hit 'em.

The sun was a small, faraway dot of yellow, but Uranus seemed to have its own light source, coming out of the sticky, pale blue mud into which they had plunged. The climate was chilly, but no worse than the Blue Ridge got during an ice storm. Granny walked around the outhouse to have a look at the damage.

It had survived pretty well for smacking into an alien planet. The wooden four-hole personal convenience had been only a few years old when Lucy had gotten the idea for launching it into space. The whole holler had turned out to reinforce it with duct tape and baling wire, and to stuff potato sacks into the crevices and corners for insulation. Mose had come up with the engine design to fuel the outhouse by attaching a modified still to it. Their first round trip, to the Moon, had been an easy journey, only it had taken more than two days on standard white lightning. The green cheese fuel had launched them out to the far expanse of the solar system in a matter of seven and a half hours. God alone knew what it would do in the tank of a bootlegger's car.

The big brass tank had been scorched dark brown by the

explosion and the flames from reentry. A hole the size of Roger's head showed where the asteroid had gone through.

"Fuel's all gone," Mose said, pursing his lips to spit.

"Now, what are we gonna do?" Granny asked.

"Meeple meep coo meep?"

Granny's reflexes had not dimmed with age. She pulled Lucy with her behind Roger. Their red shirted security officer just stood there, looking astonished at the newcomers.

They were a quartet of figures not too much taller than Granny, clad in long, enveloping black robes with hoods that threw their faces into shadow, if they had any faces.

"What do you want?" Lucy asked, peering around her cousin's protective bulk.

"Meeple meep!"

Granny felt in the pocket of her skirt. She pulled out an object and thrust it at her granddaughter.

"You can't understand alien," she said. "Use this. It's Great-great grandma Leona McFee's ear trumpet. It let her hear any kind of misbehavior from about a hundred miles away. I can still feel her slipper on my backside from taking the Lord's name in vain one time when I was ten."

The girl looked skeptically at the winding cornucopia of tin in her hands.

"You sure it'll work?"

"Honey, Grandma Leona could hear God's own angels talkin' about what to have for lunch. Give it a try."

Lucy applied it to her ear.

"Hello?" she said. "We come in peace."

"Meeble-meeble peep meeble?" asked the first hooded being.

Lucy turned to Granny. "He says, what do you call yourselves?"

"Well, we're from Earth, so I guess we're Earthlings," Granny said, after a moment's thought. "What do y'all call yourselves?"

"Meeble peep! Coo meeble gleep peep."

"He says they're Uranuseers, 'cause all they ever see is Uranus."

"Heh heh heh," Roger said. "You said Uranus."

The strangers turned their hoods toward Roger. The first being turned to Granny.

"Coo peep?"

"You got one of them, too?'" Lucy translated.

"Afraid so," Granny said. The hooded figure aimed a gloved thumb over his shoulder at the largest of the Uranuseers. The others huddled a wide step away from it. "We have to ask your pardon, Uranuseer..." Roger began to snicker again, and she gave him a look that froze him in mid-cackle. "...But we got ourselves a problem. Our ship is busted. We only meant to come and take a look at Uranus..."

"Heh heh heh."

Granny ignored Roger.

"...But we got hit by an asteroid."

"HEH HEH HEH!"

"MEEPLE!" came an answering snicker from the biggest of the Uranuseers.

Granny ignored both of them.

"Look, all we wanted to do was see what was out here, but it looks like we're stuck. If there's a place we can set up to live and maybe grow a few crops, we'd be truly grateful. We won't be no bother. And we'd be mighty glad for a chance to get to know you as neighbors."

The lead Uranuseer launched into a long series of meeps and coos. Lucy did her best to keep up.

"There's a place down south a little, near the methane lake, that y'all could settle, but it's getting into winter around here. Very soon it will be impossible to grow anything at all."

"That's bad," Roger said. "We only brought snacks along for the ride."

The lead Uranuseer seemed to sense their disappointment.

"We'd be glad to help you fix your ship. We have never seen one like it. It reminds us of a historical personal convenience for the disposal of waste fluids and solids."

"It does, does it?" Granny asked, pleased. "Looks like we all ain't so different after all."

"What's wrong with it?" Another one of the aliens stepped forward to examine it.

Mose came over to explain his design.

"...And the burner ignites a little of the gas that comes off the fermentation of the green-cheese fuel," he explained.

"Gas!" Roger cried. "Heh heh heh!"

"Meeple!"

Granny shook her head. God had made two of 'em, but thankfully He had separated them onto two different planets.

"...Only we ain't got no more green cheese to distill," Roger said. "Like Granny said, we can fix it, but can't go home without fuel. That cheese is billions of miles away on the Moon. I think we're gonna be here forever."

All of the Uranuseers went into a huddle, then broke. The lead Uranuseer turned to Granny.

"Meep peep coo meep?"

"'What about using the dirt?'" Lucy translated. She wrinkled her forehead. "What *about* the dirt?"

"Meeple meep!"

Lucy turned to Granny with the light of excitement dawning in her beautiful dark eyes.

"He says Uranus is made of blue cheese."

"You don't say," Granny said, hope rising in her heart. She looked at the ground and studied the clumps of pale mud.

Well, now that she thought about it, the blue muck did look a lot like that fancy foreign stuff that they sold in the imported foods case at Wal-Mart. Her son Zeke had brought her a tray of it for her eighty-fifth birthday. It had been pretty tasty, but she took a hairbrush to his backside for spending ten whole dollars on a pound of cheese. She took a good sniff. It stung her eyes a little, like the reek of fermentation that came off old cheese or percolating liquor. But there was no way to tell just by looking. She picked up a chunk of it and brought it up to take a taste.

"No, Granny!" Lucy said. "That could poison you!"

Granny stopped.

"You're right," she said. "Roger, you're the red shirt. Take a taste of that for me." She handed it to her grandson.

The big lug stuffed it into his mouth without ever saying grace. They all watched him as he chewed and swallowed with a big gulp, then waited nervously to see if he would keel over or not.

"Well?" Granny said at last.

"It's mighty good cheese," Roger said, licking his fingers. "We got any crackers in the lunch box?"

Granny beamed at him.

"Y'all go and help yourself, boy. We got work to do."

Together, the Uranuseers helped Roger and Lucy to repair the hole in the tank, then filled it with shovels full of the pale blue cheese. Granny made everyone stand back as Roger lighted the fire under it, but in a few minutes, thick liquid was bubbling up through the coil at the top. Roger leaned in the door of the outhouse and came back with a big grin.

"All powered up, Granny—I mean, Captain. I think it's gonna blast us back home in about three hours flat!"

Granny put out her hand and grasped the sleeve of the lead Uranuseer.

"I gotta thank you for all of your help. I hope we can come back again sometime soon and really see Uranus."

"HEH HEH HEH," Roger laughed, slapping his thigh with his hand. "HEH HEH HEH!"

"MEEPLE!" the big alien boomed.

"Meeple gleep meep?" the lead Uranuseer asked, in a plaintive tone.

Granny didn't wait for Lucy to translate.

"Sorry," Granny said. "It's only a four-holer, and I don't think Earth is ready for both of 'em at once."

"Meeple," the lead Uranuseer said in resignation.

Granny shooed her family back into the outhouse, waved farewell to their new friends, and shut the door.

"All right," she said, wriggling her rear into place on the wooden seat. "Ready to take off?"

"Ready, Granny!" Roger and Lucy chorused. Granny clutched the wheel.

"Let's leave Uranus behind!"

"Heh heh heh!" Roger laughed until tears ran down his big broad face. "You said..."

"Shut up!" Granny snapped. "Blast off!"

Jody Lynn Nye lists her main career activity as "spoiling cats." She lives northwest of Chicago with one of the above and her husband, author and packager Bill Fawcett. She has written over forty books, including *The Ship Who Won* with Anne McCaffrey, eight books with Robert Asprin, a humorous anthology about mothers, *Don't Forget Your Spacesuit, Dear!*, and over 140 short stories. Her latest books are *Rhythm of the Imperium* (Baen Books), *Wishing On a Star* (Arc Manor Publishing), and *Myth-Fits* (Ace Books). Jody also reviews fiction for *Galaxy's Edge* magazine and teaches the intensive writers' workshop at DragonCon.

The Way of the Jedy
Gloria Oliver

Maribelle ducked into an old drainage pipe gaping at her out of the darkness. Half bent over and cradling her shotgun, she scooted backwards into the pipe and the smelly, stagnant water trapped inside it. With any luck, it would cover her scent enough to lose the yumbies on her tail.

She should have known better than to listen to Ned. This mess was all his fault! The fool—going on and on about the store dummies he'd seen while exploring and their pretty dresses. How she should go get her one to be dressed up lady like for the summer social an' all.

Momma had been strongly hintin' she needed to find herself a man and start a family—to do her part to save the human race. Maribelle hadn't been so sure, but it sounded so important the way Momma said it.

So double fool she for getting fancy ideas and listening to Ned. All the rotgut must have made him half blind, for the dummies hadn't been dummies at all, but damn yumbies posing 'cause they had to vogue.

Maribelle put her hand over her mouth and tried to calm herself, her labored breathing echoing way too loud in the confined space. She only had two shotgun shells left—or only one if she kept the promise she'd made to herself of using one to plug Ned's pie hole. But she still had a couple of miles to go to get to safety and a whole lot of hungry things still shambling out there. What was she gonna do?

The sounds of snapping twigs and mindless moaning drifted in from outside making her shiver. She scrunched down lower, her back and knees protesting, trying to make herself as small as she could.

An odd humming reverberated nearby, a sound she didn't think she'd ever heard before. It seemed to wax and wane, as if moving back and forth. Flashes of light reflected in the stagnant water from the outside, and they matched the odd humming sound.

Then something dropped inside the pipe and rolled into

the water in her direction. Maribelle tried to scooch even farther back, but the pipe narrowed, leaving her nowhere else to go. The thing came to a stop and a partially decomposed face with rheumy eyes leered at her, chomping its chops.

Dang it! She kicked the thing right back out to where it'd come from. Were the yumbies fighting with one another to see who would get to eat her first? They better think again if they thought she'd be easy pickings.

"Oh, there you are!"

A stick of light stabbed down into the head just outside the pipe entrance. The smell of cooking rotten flesh wafted in making her gag as the stench worked its way down her throat and lungs.

"Miss, you can come out now. It's safe."

Yeah right, like she'd been born yesterday. Yumbies weren't much to look at, but sometimes they were crafty. She knew all about the trick they pulled in Troy County with a giant fake can of beer they hid themselves in until some poor unsuspecting souls wheeled it into their compound. These dead buggers held nothing sacred. Nothing at *all*.

A long, glowing blue stick with electrodes at the end brought some light into the pipe and a young man's face peered in. Unlike the last one, this face was whole and might actually be alive.

"I'm a Jedy, Miss. Jebediah Jedy. And I'm here to rescue you." A pleased puppy smile lit up his face as if he'd been waiting for a chance to say that for ages.

Maribelle snorted before she could stop herself. He thought he was doing what? "I can take care of myself, thankyouverymuch."

"I'm sure that's right, Miss. But now you'll have an easier time doing it."

Was he poking fun at her? He had a little bit of a funny accent. Guess she had no choice but to try and find out. "Just backup and stay where I can see you."

"As you wish." He stepped backwards slowly, leaving his weird stick pointing down so she would have a little light to see by.

Maribelle inched forward, the barrel of her shotgun pointed right at him throughout. Her back and knees complained louder than before as she came out of the pipe and straightened. She paid them no mind, though, instead ogling at what she couldn't see before.

There were yumbie parts *everywhere*. Some quick finger counting and figuring came up with at least five zombies littering the area. And he'd done this alone? Dang...

Trying to keep her expression neutral, Maribelle pointed the barrel of the shotgun at the ground and turned her full attention on her rescuer and the weapon which had had such an impact on the yumbies. The stick was a two and a half footer. Its central shaft held a coiled tube of some sort running its length, which was where the blue glow came from. An acrylic sheath covered it and it had two blades pinned in grooves cut into the clear substance. At the top, the shaft split in two and ended in cattle prod electrodes. As she watched, a tiny bolt of lightning danced for a moment between the two.

As for Jedy, he was shorter than she'd reckoned, five one tops. And he dressed funny. His clothes wrapped around him like layers of bath robes and he had a hooded cloak that looked much too large. But silly as he looked, the severed pieces of zombie around him told a different story.

"How, could you take on so many by yourself and live?"

He looked sheepish for a moment as if embarrassed a little by the question. Not your typical reaction at all. Heck, all the single yahoos at camp would have puffed out their chests and boasted it was nothing. As if.

"It's because I follow the ways of the Farce." He stood ramrod straight as he said this, his expression serious. "I'm a Jedy, like my father before me. It's what we do."

This was sounding weirder by the second. "The ways of the Farce?"

He nodded. "The Farce is all around us. Life creates it, makes it grow. Its energy surrounds and binds us. They used to be a part of it too, but now they're not." He nodded towards the pieces of dead zombies around them. "They took the easy path and are now lost."

Maribelle shook her head not quite catching his meaning. There was a lot of mystery in what had happened to the world and why it all went to shit, but she didn't think his explanation was it. "Uh, sure. Well, thanks for the help. But I probably should get going now."

"No! Please don't."

She brought the barrel of her shotgun back up. "Why the hell not? You think I should be giving you some kind of reward or something?"

Jebediah took a step back, giving her space. "No, of course not! It's just that, won't you let me walk with you? To make sure you get home safe? I've felt… a disturbance in the Farce. It… it isn't safe for anyone to be out alone tonight."

Maribelle sighed. Was that really all there was to it? She didn't get the usual vibe from this one, but you always had to be on your guard. Still… "I supposed it would be prudent. At least for a little ways."

Jebediah nodded eagerly, making him look like a puppy again. Maribelle did like puppies.

She nodded and moved to join him.

"We were destined to meet, you and I."

She rolled her eyes at the obvious lie. Maybe she didn't like puppies quite so much after all. "Is that right?"

"I've dreamt about you often, Maribelle."

She stopped in her tracks, her finger automatically moving to rest on the shotgun's trigger. He knew her *name*. How could he know *her name*?

"I've spoken to you in my dreams many times. I knew where you were going to be, I saw the danger you would be in. How else do you think I knew to come rescue you?"

Huh. Could that be true? Her Momma had been talking a lot about Pa lately, how the two of them had been soul mates? Maribelle had never known him. Hadn't ever had much need for any man. But could such things be true? Could people be that connected?

To her surprise, Maribelle found her heart beating just a little faster at the thought, her cheeks feeling warm. And it wasn't even from being scared or running from yumbies neither. She slid a sideways glance at Jebediah.

He really wasn't all that bad lookin' once you got used to the bathrobes. And he seemed to be smart and strong, a sight better than the choices at camp, even if he seemed a little touched in the head.

She might not have been able to get a nice dress, but maybe, just maybe, she'd found something even better. Maribelle hitched up her halter top, thinking this trip might not be such a waste after all.

It might even be time to bring a boy home to meet her Momma.

After the couple moved on, a lone fist rose up out of a bush of poison ivy and pumped the air three times amidst muffled giggles. Minutes later, a solitary figure rose from the depths of the bush. He was covered from head to toe in black and wore a spray painted black bucket with two punched out holes on his head like a helmet.

Yes, sir—another man eating woman crossed off the list. Another ball and chain avoided.

Ned pulled out a flashlight covered in red saranwrap and turned it on. Then he dug into his knapsack rummaging through his collections of DVDs for a likely candidate to use as inspiration for how to deal with the next name on his list. "Silence of the Lambs"—ah, yes, *Clarice*...that surely had some possibilities.

The Farce was clearly with him.

The End

Gloria Oliver lives in Texas making sure to stay away from rolling tumbleweeds while bowing to the never ending wishes of her feline and canine masters.

She is the author of *In the Service of Samurai*, *Vassal of El*, *Cross-eyed Dragon Troubles*, *Willing Sacrifice*, *The Price of Mercy*, *Inner Demons*, and *Jewel of the Gods*. The novels are fantasy, young adult fantasy, and urban fantasy (notice a pattern?), several with romantic elements.

She is a member in good standing of EPIC, BroadUniverse, SASS, and Future Classics (ask us about our antho!), though she has yet to make the list for Cat Slaves R Us.

For free reads, sample chapters, social media links, and more info, please drop by and visit her at <www.gloriaoliver.com>, or see what's she's up to at <blog.gloriaoliver.com>.

Dark Matter Degree
Morris Reban

Graduates, faculty, and honored guests, as the Dean of the College of Sanitation Astrophysics, allow me to welcome you to this, our commencement ceremony of 2633 C.E.

Humanity's understanding of the physical nature of the universe has continued to increase, based on laws and principles first discovered, in large part, during the 20th and 21st centuries.

An oft-forgotten part of this understanding derived from what seemed, at the time, one of the most unlikely of origins. During the 20th century, a form of recreational enterprise was created: that of taking an entertaining voyage on the oceans and other bodies of water on the planet Earth. This was called "taking a cruise" and was done by purchasing accommodations on a "cruise ship," a vessel usually designed specifically for concentrating large numbers of people into small, cramped personal compartments, so as to encourage them to exit often, and enjoy extremely overpriced and overcrowded entertainments aboard the "cruise ship," such as climbing an artificial rock wall, this being a common reason to travel at sea.

During this same period, elsewhere on Earth, astrophysicists were noticing that the estimates they were making of mass for galaxies and larger structures using dynamic and general relativistic methods were much greater than what they were finding of the actual mass of the visible "luminous" matter. Their calculations indicated that the total substance of the universe amounted to only 4.9% ordinary matter, while dark matter amounted to 26.8% and dark energy 68.3%, a total dark mass of 95.1% of the mass of the universe.

It was therefore the question of the era to be answered: what was this dark mass and from whence did it originate?

It was not until the late 21st century that Professor Irwin Coreywine of the University of Ganymede proposed a viable theory. It was based, of all things, on those "cruise ships," and he developed it from his experience as an impoverished young student during a working sabbatical on Earth, while employed on such a vessel. He noticed that there was an increasing number of complaints from various ports along the voyages of such ships. The ships would stop at harbors on various islands and seashores to allow brief sojourns on land for the passengers, while the ship's crew mopped up the results of over-rich food and seasickness. The waters just outside these harbors were, in fact, becoming increasingly noxious and polluted. This, it turned out, was due to the ships dumping the contents of their sanitation systems holding tanks before entering the harbors, so that passengers would be unlikely to notice the stench as they came and went ashore. It also avoided local regulations as to how such material should be handled while actually in the harbor.

This accumulated nearby, however, over many voyages and vessels, and caused a disruption in the ecologies nearby the harbors, as well as an increasing stench blown in by atmospheric activity, known as "sea breezes."

This, therefore, gave Professor Coreywine the essential clue for the origin of dark mass. In the millions of years of the existence of the Universe, the same commercial activity, substituting space for planetary bodies of water, had been taking place in the millions of advanced space-faring civilizations. The same procedure was followed by uncounted spacecraft of innumerable species, which dumped their holding tanks into the increasingly polluted space near the planets along their routes. Given the wide variation in different species effluvia, this resulted in the various sub-classifications of dark matter, such as "Hot", being very fresh; "Warm", being solid and/or sticky, and of course, "Cold", referring to hard lumps.

As an additional inspiration, Professor Coreywine also retrieved a principle created by a 20th century science fiction writer, one Theodore Sturgeon, who stated that "Using the same standards that categorize 90% of science fiction as trash, crud, or crap, it can be argued that 90% of film, literature, consumer goods, etc. is crap." Coreywine was able to prove, mathematically extrapolating from this brilliant insight, that in reality, 95.1% of everything is crap, or dark matter.

And because of this, the science of sanitation astrophysics has become an honorable and essential part of the civilizations of the universe. So, today, as we grant final degrees to our dedicated graduates, I say to you, new sanitation astrophysicists go forth into the universe and clean up that dark matter.

And thank you all for coming.

Morris Reban is a *nom de plume** used for writing fiction by someone who takes the term "Flush fiction" far too literally. One guy, two replaced joints, a pair of aging cats, and a very disorganized workshop, so it's amazing he actually got a story in YDP's *I Didn't Quite Make It to Oz.*

* *nom de plume* (freely translated from the French for "eat the feather")

Greeter by Day; Skeeters by Night
Selina Rosen

"Ya don' understand, Brian, I ain't trin' ta be difficult I jus'… well I cain't work at night that's all," Dan said.

"I'm sorry, Dan, it's out of my hands."

Well that was a load of crap and Dan knew it. That still-wet-behind-the-ears piece of shit was one of the department managers. Dan glared after Brian's departing form. Dan had been a door greeter at Wal-Mart for over two years, ever since he'd been forced into retirement. He sure didn't want to give up his job, but he just couldn't work nights. He couldn't help it, he didn't ask to be cursed, but he guessed he maybe shouldn't have slept with that voodoo witch's daughter; things sure hadn't been the same since.

He saw Brian whispering to the store manager and knew what it meant that they kept looking over at him. The bastards were just trying to get him to quit, most probably had a grandfather they wanted to give the job to. Well he hadn't ever quit a job in his life and he wouldn't start now.

The big boss started over and Dan inwardly cringed.

"Brian tells me you won't change shifts."

"Ain't ah question of won', Tom. I cain't, I gots me a medical condition."

Tom laughed. "Now Dan we both know that isn't true. It would have said something in your files. Now you just be here at six tomorrow evening or you can turn in your smock right now."

Dan glared at Tom. "Oh I'll be here, and you'll be powerful sorry."

Dan showed up for work at six the next day and Brian walked over to him whistling. "Well I see you're here."

"Yep."

"And you haven't turned into a pillar of salt yet."

"It ain't quite dark yet, and I don' turn inta salt ya pecker head." Just then the sun finished going down and a buzzing started to come from Dan's cheeks and his belly. "I turn inta skeeters, dumb ass, an' I ain't sure but we might have the West Nile, and we're immune to Deet, so ya best get ta runnin'."

Selina Rosen is the author of over twenty-five novels including *Sword Masters* and *Strange Robby*, and she has had dozens of short stories published in professional venues including *Thieves World* and *Impossible Monsters*. As editor-in-chief of Yard Dog Press she has edited *ten* anthologies including *Bubbas of the Apocalypse*. She is married, owns a small farm, and has kids and grandkids. She is a carpenter, a rock mason, a sword fighter and an all-around swell gal. Check out her titles at <selinarosen.com> or friend her on Facebook.

Stranded at the Gates of Hell
Susan Satterfield

Harold was hot, tired and on the verge of losing his mind. It had not been a good day. As a matter of fact, it was literally the day from hell.

"What do you mean you can't find my records?" Harold blurted out before realizing who he was talking to.

The demon perched behind the large, shiny black desk shrugged his scaly shoulders.

"Hey bub, nobody's perfect! Even us supernatural beings can have an off day. Besides, nuthin's been the same since those bozos downstairs decided to computerize." Its glowing red eyes flashed in anger as it bashed the side of the monitor, whose heavily insulated case showed scars of previous abuse. "They expect us to learn how 'ta use these things after just one class by some third level demon who couldn't tell a computer from brimstone, even after smelling the sulphur." The creature was getting more frustrated with each key he punched. "Besides I think there's something wrong with the program. It has so many bugs, we should call an exterminator. I tried to tell'em we needed technical support, but they wouldn't listen ta me! After all, I'm just some poor schmuck tryin' to earn my way through the afterlife."

Harold rolled his eyes in exasperation. His usually carefully styled, thick blond hair was plastered against his head. Sweat poured down his face, leaving streaks of soot.

"So you're telling me I'm stranded?"

The demon appeared almost sympathetic.

"I don't know what to tell ya. Until this hunk of shit decides to spit up your records we can't let you in."

"I DON'T WANT TO GO IN!" Harold's patience was at an end. "I shouldn't be down here at all. I was a GOOD person. I loved my wife, even when she nagged me unmercifully. I never beat my children. I was a reliable, honest worker at a job I didn't particularly want. Every Sunday, I was in church. I was even a virgin when I got married, how many men can say that?"

"Whoa, blue eyes! I know this and you know this, but the computer don't. Like I told ya before, you'll just haveta wait. I've got three lesser demons and two succubi searching our records by claw. We've even contacted the ambassador from goody two-shoes land, and they even agreed ta search from their end. Until we find those records, I suggest you plant your bony butt on that bench over there and wait; this may take a while."

Harold glared at the demon, who waved to the next soul in line.

"Next," the demon bellowed, a small spurt of flame issuing from each nostril.

Harold threw up his hands and stomped over to a marble bench against a nearby wall. Even though the seat was hot, Harold was too upset to notice. This day had gone from bad to worse. The last thing he clearly remembered was sitting in his office, his chest exploding in terrible pain and trying to get to the phone to call for help. The next thing he knew he was standing in a long line, winding through a series of hot, humid caverns. The people standing around him seemed to be in some sort of trance. He had tried to talk to those nearest, but he may as well have been talking to statues. They didn't even acknowledge his existence. He had no idea where he was or how he had gotten there until he made it to the front of the line and saw that smart ass demon sitting behind the desk.

Harold leaned against the wall and closed his eyes. He reran his life, looking for something he had done to deserve such a fate, but came up empty. The only thing he could figure out was that maybe he'd been too much of a wimp.

A loud crash, followed by a stream of extremely colorful curses beginning with something being filled with a load of batshit startled Harold out of his daydream. The demon had thrown his computer on the red carpeted floor and was doing his best to beat the machine into submission. Harold got up from his bench, wandered over and leaned casually against the creature's desk.

"Problem?"

The demon stopped and shot him a look of pure, unadulterated evil.

"I HATE computers!"

Harold thought it over for a minute. He was not only an excellent computer programmer, but had also taken several courses in computer repair and maintenance. He might as well help, it would be a good way to pass the time and might even enable him to find his records and get out of here as quickly as possible.

"Look, uh, whatever your name is..."

"Belal."

"Well, Belal, I know quite a bit about computers, maybe I can do something about it."

Belal stared at him, but finally stepped to one side and motioned toward the machine.

"Might as well let you give it a try, I sure can't get this god-spawned, heap of angel crap to work."

Harold walked over and picked up the computer, carefully replacing it on the desk and sat down in front of the recalcitrant machine.

"Hey, Hal! Hurry every chance ya git. They've got us on a weird ass time-management program, and I can't afford ta get too far behind on my quota."

Harold nodded absently and dove right into his work. He had always liked working with computers; in many ways he much preferred the company of machines to that of people. He had almost forgotten how much fun he had working with them. Harold hadn't wanted to take the supervisory position his company had offered him, but his wife had nagged him into it. It was much easier to give into her than it was to listen to her complain all the time. She wouldn't even let him get a home computer, saying she had better things for him to do with his time and money than messing with such an expensive toy. Harold suddenly realized he was having the time of his life. Finally, he sat back with a sigh of contentment.

"Belal, it's fixed," he called, feeling very self-satisfied.

The demon flew into the room and landed with a rush of hot air beside him.

"Alright, Harold! You just saved my tail."

Harold smiled in wonder. He couldn't remember the last time he had felt so good. It had been great working with computers again and knowing he hadn't lost his touch.

Belal quickly entered a name and breathed a fiery sigh of relief when the correct information appeared on the screen.

"This is great! Boy, I wish I could keep ya around to help. You're the first soul I've found who can make these halo-riddled things work. Seems all the other experts are too involved with their machines to sin enough to warrant transfer here."

Harold paused and thought hard for minute. *Why not,* he thought. He certainly could imagine worse ways to spend eternity, besides he thoroughly enjoyed the idea of being able to play with his machines without having to deal with the constant nagging.

"Sounds like a game plan to me," Harold responded, "but of course I have a few requests. First, I want an air conditioned room to work in." He knew one of the first things he would have to do is figure out some way to keep the computers cool at each workstation, but he wanted a cool place to rest too. "Second, I'll need someone to fetch parts and stuff."

Belal squealed with impish glee. "I'll get you a flunky right away!" He paused. This was going to be a good one to explain to his royal hotness, but for the moment, Belal didn't care. He had Harold and would do anything to keep him. Belal grabbed Harold's arm and towed him to the next station where a seductive young succubi was preparing to deposit her computer against the nearest wall.

A smile covered Harold's face as he gently relieved the surprised creature of her burden and began his afterlife in his own slice of heaven. Hell wasn't going to be too bad after all!

—The End—

Susan Satterfield is the author of a number of published short stories and poems including "The Lady Killer" and "Sweet Teddy" which appeared in an anthology entitled *Small Bites.* Her Yard Dog stories include "What Goes Around" (*Flush Fiction) and* "A Bad Case of the Munchies" (*I Should Have Stayed in Oz).* Her poem entitled "The Hunger: A Zombie Poem" was published by Costcom. She also has a novella with Yard Dog Press entitled *Mirror Images.*

Currently, Susan teaches online, hybrid, and traditional courses including composition, creative writing, and Introduction to Literature at MCC-Longview Community College. She lives in Lee's Summit, Missouri with her family including dogs and an ornery black cat.

A Dark Bird
Bradley H. Sinor

She closed the book, placed it on the table and, finally, decided to walk through the door. The words of the poems echoed in her head.

She hesitated for only a moment before crossing the threshold, as the blue flames wrapped around her, sending a tingling cold into the deepest bits of her.

For the longest time there was nothing. Finally in the distance came the sound of water gently lapping against the piers of a dock, the cold December winds reaching out onto the water. A dark bird of her desire circled near her.

"The one you seek is near," said the creature.

Two men in the heavy jackets and caps of seamen shivered as she passed, one crossing himself and drawing deeper within his jacket. The other crossed himself, glancing up into the sky at the full moon.

"Why do you torment me?" she asked the bird.

The creature landed atop a broken hitching rail. The top bore a slight resemblance to a man's head. It preened the ink dark feathers, then looked at her.

"You are the one who torments yourself, pulling yourself here beyond the barriers of time and space and desire. You found his words, his dreams and you want him, you want him as a part of yourself; but you can't have him, you know that as well as I," said the bird.

In the distance was a tolling bell, marking the hour. The house she found herself standing in front of was small, two stories. She saw the small plate near the door, 203 Amity Street. The dark bird circled and landed on her shoulder.

It took her a long time before she could make herself reach up and rap on the door, three soft sounds and then nothing. For what seemed like hours she stood silently, watching the door; the sounds of the city distant even here.

When no answer to her knock came, she found herself walking into the house without invitation. The dark bird on her shoulder murmured sounds into her ear as she moved into the room and saw him.

He sat slumped in a worn leather chair, a pile of ancient volumes spread at his feet.

"Are you here, or do I dream again?" he asked without looking toward her.

"I am here," she replied. "As for dreaming, who can say if this is your dream, mine or perhaps someone else's?"

"Yet each time you come you take a bit of my soul with you when you leave," he said. The dark bird made the leap from her shoulder to the arm of his chair, then flitted over to a bust that stood in the corner of the room. "Why do you torment me, Lenore? You know I have loved you, but you are always beyond my reach."

"And you beyond mine," she said, leaning forward to let her lips brush his cheek. "Goodbye, Edgar."

Then, before he could speak, she turned and went back through the door. Outside the house a man in a long cape, white scarf and dark hat, with three roses and a bottle of cognac in his hand, stood. He offered her his arm. A moment later blue flames wrapped around them as the two walked on.

The man in the house remained unmoving in his chair as the distant church bell tolled midnight. He finally bestirred himself, taking a sheet of paper, a pen in his hand and began to write, speaking each word as his pen moved.

"Once upon a midnight dreary...."

Bradley Sinor has been writing for five/sixths of his life, and has written many short stories, most of them published in a variety of anthologies and three short story collections. He lives in Tulsa, OK, with his wife (writer and copy-editor) Sue Sinor and four cats.

Crocaroo
Sue Sinor

Have you ever seen a crocaroo? Yes, a crocaroo. At least, that's what I call what I saw last summer. What, you say, IS a crocaroo? Let me tell you a story.

My Uncle Beezer and I were hunting in southern Louisiana last summer. We were somewhere to the east of Grand Bayou, hunting for whatever was edible and legal.

"Jimmy," Uncle Beezer said, "Look over yonder. What does that look like to you?"

I looked. "Looks like a jackrabbit to me. A big one. What does it look like to you?"

"Well, for a minute it looked a little like a kangaroo, but with a strange looking head." He stared for another moment. "Yeah, I guess you're right. We don't really have 'roos around here."

We walked on, looking for deer or squirrels or whatever we'd have for supper. Possums would be okay, too, but we didn't see any of those, either.

"Jimmy," my uncle said suddenly, "Do you believe in Sasquatches?"

Now, I knew my uncle had some strange ideas. He believed in monsters and astrology and ghosts, things like that, so it didn't surprise me that he asked me that question.

"I've never seen one, so I can't say yes, but I've never seen a lot of things that I know exists, either. Why do you ask?"

He looked around for a moment without saying anything, then, "Jimmy, I've been thinking about going up to Washington state for a while to look for one."

We walked on. "How would you get there? You don't drive."

"Oh, I can drive. I just prefer to have other people take me where I need to go. Like you."

"You've got to be kidding!" I stopped in my tracks and faced him. "I've been taking you places for years, thinking you couldn't drive, and now you tell me that. Don't you dare ask me for a ride again."

"But I don't have a car," he whined.

"And whose fault is that? I saved up to get the junker I drive. It was all I could afford with my crappy job."

"Yeah, it is a junker, all right. But have I ever complained? Of course not. It's your car."

"Well, now you can buy your own car to take you where you want to go. I quit!"

I stomped off, leaving him to think about what I said. That's when I heard him yell.

"Jimmy! Watch out!"

I turned and saw the scariest thing I've ever seen not five feet from me. It had the body of what looked like a kangaroo, but its head was shaped like a crocodile's head, with rows of razor-sharp teeth. I stood frozen, trying to make sense of it. Fortunately, Beezer thought faster than I did and ran toward me swinging his rifle.

He whopped that thing upside the head, which only made it look at him.

"Run!" I yelled to him. I raised my rifle and looked through the site. I couldn't get a clear shot, so I started running, too.

Beezer started running in a zigzag pattern to confuse the critter, and when he found a suitable tree, he climbed it as far as he could get.

But the damned thing could jump. It tried to catch him by jumping up the tree, but I got close enough to get a bead on it and fired. I don't think I hit it, but I scared it. It started hopping away toward the bayou and we hightailed it back to my car. We decided that take-out would do for supper, and the next time we went hunting, we'd go to Arkansas.

"You know," I mused. "If I'd killed that thing, we coulda had crockpot roo for dinner."

The End

Sue Sinor has several short stories and two chapbooks (*Playing With Secrets* and *Bubba Fables*) published by Yard Dog Press, as-well-as a story in *Grantville Gazette 41* and one in the DAW anthology *Rotten Relations*, both written with husband Brad. They live in Tulsa, OK, with four cats. You can find her on Facebook.

Field Test No. 421
Allison Stein

Our investigation into the secret passages below Evelyn's family's office tower continues. Evelyn and I found evidence of recent excavation in the tunnel we discovered yesterday. We returned today with equipment more suited to subterranean exploration.

Today also marked the first field test of my new personal transportation device, the design of which I based on the mechanical spiders that attacked us last week. Luckily, I managed to save a few of the little metal beasties for study before Evelyn smashed them all.

Their design is quite ingenious! I scaled up the size to accommodate a human of my size and weight and *viola!*— an eight-legged personal transportation device that handles uneven terrain better than any of my multi-wheeled devices. It was quite suitable for chasing the unknown down dark passageways and, with a few modifications, it will adequately handle vertical surfaces as well. Anticipating its use on rough terrain, I installed an overstuffed velvet chair trimmed with silk tassels and carved walnut accents. I also installed restraining straps to go across my waist and over both shoulders, crisscrossing in front. The chair's placement on the middle of what would otherwise be the arachnid's cephalothorax provided excellent stability atop the device's eight jointed legs. (Note to self: Before attempting to scale a vertical wall again, add gimbals to the chair mount.)

Other improvements include six directional lamps and a device of my own invention that squirts a fast-drying compound with the strength, versatility, and adhesion of spider's silk. For purely defensive purposes, I've installed a device that fires darts loaded with a compound similar to spider venom. It will sting like the dickens and incapacitate the target for a few minutes but cause no lasting health concerns.

Evelyn and I rendezvoused at the tunnel entrance and inventoried our equipment. In addition to my transportation device, I brought flashlights, ropes, and grapples. Evelyn brought fresh ginger snaps and a canteen of sweet tea.

"In case we get a bit peckish," she said. "Or lost."

"I never get lost," I reminded her.

"Oh, really? You just keep believing that, Mary," she replied.

With our equipment sorted and our intentions set, we proceeded into the tunnel. My lamps only illuminated a few yards into the darkness. (Note to self: Upgrade the lumen output of the existing lamps, or add more of them.)

Water dripped somewhere in the darkness. Evelyn hopped back and forth over the rivulet of dark liquid that ran down the middle of the passage. Our every step echoed: the tippity-tap of each of my device's eight legs and the shuffling of Evelyn's soft leather loafers. The tunnel reeked of mold, earth, rot, sewer gas, and something unknown but decidedly dead. Whether it was a rat, raccoon, or something ... *larger* ... I couldn't say. With pinched noses, we pressed onward and downward into the smelly darkness.

Evelyn stopped and dropped into a crouch, clearly on the edge of something dark, deep, and most certainly dangerous.

"Mary! Shine a lamp over here," she whispered.

I aimed my lamps where she pointed, revealing a steeply-canted stairway descending into the darkness below. I considered it with my scientist's objectivity. "It looks dangerous and terribly steep. You go first," I said.

"Really?" she asked. "You're the one with the lamps!"

"But you are the natural born explorer. I'm merely the observer," I reminded her.

"Right then. Onward!" she said. Standing, she hiked up her pants and began her descent.

At the bottom of the stairs, Evelyn stumbled, grabbing at the wall to prevent an awkward fall. Something in the darkness beneath her hand gave way with a shriek of metal against metal long past the need of a good oiling, then stone scraped against stone. The wall moved aside, revealing a chamber filled with row upon row of metal men, each with a cable sprouting from its chest and connected to a bank of electrical power stations. Row after row, the metal men emitted a steady electric hum, the identical eyes in their identical faces glowing.

"Yikes!" Evelyn squeaked.

"Brilliant!" I exclaimed. "My father's journals mentioned designs for a robot army, but didn't mention they had actually been built."

I examined a metal man in more detail. "Battery powered. Fully charged. They're ready to use! They should be voice activated. Go ahead, Evie! Give them a command."

"Me?" she asked. "Your father designed them."

"Well, yes. But he designed them for YOUR father," I replied. "Besides, you have a natural rapport with large groups."

Evelyn smiled. "I know, right?"

With two perfectly synchronized clanks of their metal feet, the metal men turned to face right.

"Wait! I didn't do that, did I? I take it back! Turn around!"

The metal men turned 180 degrees to face left, stamping their metal feet in unison.

"Oh, never mind! Forget I said anything. Come on, Mary! The passage continues at the back of this room."

Evelyn set off out of the room and down the passage. I followed her, and the phalanx of metal men clanking along behind us.

"Oh, bother!" Evelyn sighed.

The second passage opened into an immense, well-lit room. Evelyn's stepmother Matilda stood in the center of it, a martini in one hand and a raygun pistol in the other.

"Hello, Evelyn. And Mary!" She gestured at the metal men behind us. "I heard you coming."

"Ah, well, sorry about that." Evelyn said. She craned her neck to get a better look at the room's architectural detail. Matilda must have an army of master stone carvers on her secret payroll. It was all quite impressive.

"So very naughty of you, finding my secret lair," Matilda said. "Every villain needs a secret lair, don't you agree? Take a good look around. This room will be the last thing you see." She made a noise that was one part schoolgirl giggle and two parts terrifying chuckle.

Evelyn sniffed. "Laughter doesn't become you, Stepmother. Your threats don't scare me anymore."

"Don't be so petulant. I know we've had our differences since your father disappeared, but let's end on a positive note, shall we? Come take a look around. I've been dying to show it off! That's the problem with secret lairs. You can't invite anyone over, because it's supposed to be a secret!"

She gestured with her raygun. "Over here we have the armory and ammunitions locker; down the hall we have the crypt for the zombies. You've already found my robot army. Aren't they charming? I modeled them on your father. Note the regal profile." She gestured, as if modeling a new cosmetic.

"Oh, and by the way: my voice commands override all others. Didn't think of that, did you? Sorry, dear. Sucks to be you."

Evelyn bristled. "What are you going to do with all of this, Stepmother?"

"Don't you worry about that. Life's short, remember? I promised myself I would never monologue about my secret plans. That's always the first step toward failure. But I'm just so excited by what I've accomplished here! These tunnels can withstand an earthquake, and the temperature is perfect for storing both the zombies and a long-term food supply. I've tapped into the city's power grid, but you've probably figured that out already. I have on some exciting new ideas for alternate power sources, should the need arise. But there I go, monologuing again. Let's move on, shall we? Let me show you the entertainment room..."

When Matilda turned to leave the room, I saw my chance and took it. I charged forward in my spider-like device, firing the darts to incapacitate her and spraying the sticky spider web goo to bind her. Matilda yelped in a most unflattering way, then sank into unconsciousness, stuck to the cold stone floor.

Evelyn faced the metal men. "Robots! I alone command you now!" she shouted. "Carry her upstairs to the building lobby. The security guard will call the police."

"Right!" I agreed. "And if I know the police, and I do, they'll get her to confess to her role in your father's disappearance. We just might find him yet!"

Evelyn smiled and opened her mouth to speak, then stopped with a strange expression on her face. "Did Matilda say something about zombies?"

Allison Stein is an artist, author, TV addict, geek princess, and cat servant—not necessarily in that order. Her award-winning short fiction and cover illustrations have been published by Yard Dog Press and several other small presses.

She is a founding member the NobleFusion writers' collective. By day, she is a writer/editor specializing in technical documentation that even technophobes can understand. When not painting, writing, updating her social media status, or serving as cat furniture, she hoards art supplies and practices Advanced Google-Fu. | AllisonStein.com | @allisonstein |

Confessions of a Husband Beater

Katherine A. Turski

I beat my husband the other night. I couldn't help it; he asked for it.

"I'm tired of playing games," I said. "How much more do you think you can take?"

"Come on," he coaxed. "Just one more round of Battleship."

He shouldn't have pushed me like that. After the third beating he reeled slightly, blinking in bewilderment.

"How can you do that?" Staring at the ships on the computer screen, he added, "I can't even find your aircraft carrier. What kind of goofy strategy are you using?"

"It's called 'hide the ships where you can't find them'."

"That's ridiculous. I should be able to find them all." This is from a man who demands daily where I've hidden his reading glasses. "You must be cheating."

He shouldn't have accused me of cheating. I demolished his fleet three more times. Even his PT boat wasn't safe.

"Just a few more rounds," he mumbled.

"Haven't you had enough punishment?"

He shook his head. "Are you kidding? I'm just getting warmed up. What, are you scared of losing?"

"I've been petrified the whole time."

"Very funny. Come on, set up for the next round."

I put a hand on his shoulder and said softly, "It's late, honey, we need to get to sleep." Once the lights were out, I pretended not to hear him whimper, "Just one more round". I felt like a sadist.

For the rest of the week he begged me for more. I only replied, "Not tonight, I have a headache."

Several nights later we visited another couple. After dinner they invited us to play games. My husband's face paled and he excused himself to the restroom, claiming a possible case of distemper. The wife gave me a look eloquent with sympathy.

"You beat you husband, don't you?"

"Only at Battleship. He asks for it, though."

"They always do." She stared at the husband, who fiddled

nervously with a card deck. "Try beating this one at Scrabble. He'll keep you up all night until he finally wins. The tiles are so stained with sweat you can't read the letters anymore."

"And the dictionary?"

She shuddered. "Don't ask."

Ads for popular games claim their products bring people closer together. So does hand to hand combat.

Yet, after much thought and research, I've finally found the perfect game for my husband and me to enjoy. There will be no more complaining, no suspicion of cheating, no criticizing strategy. I call it "Strip Twister". The way I figure it, my husband will never know if he's winning or losing, and even if he does, he probably won't care.

Kathy Turski writes the way she looks—short and funny. She lives in North Texas with her husband, and clerks in a public library in order to serve her feline overlords. When she has any spare time, she enjoys corny old movies, baking, and of course, writing. Some of Kathy's stories are published with Yard Dog's *A Bubba In Time Saves None, Anthology From Hell*, and she has an illustrated novella, *It's the Great Bumpkin, Cletus Brown* (Cover & interior illustrations by Sherri Dean).

Oh, and never, ever stand between her and a cheesecake unless your insurance is paid up.

COUGAR
Laura J. Underwood

Jack was cleaning glasses when the young man wandered into the bar and crawled onto a stool. He started looking around at the usual crowd that held court in Kelly's Corner as if seeking a target. Jack managed to keep a smile off his face. *Desperate, are we?*

Yeah, he had seen that look too many times before. He walked down the bar and stopped in front of the young man.

"Can I help you?"

"Whatever's on tap," the young man said.

Jack nodded and went back up the bar and drew a pint of beer. The young man continued to look around until he spied Eleanor over in the corner. As usual, she was wearing something so alluring, it was a wonder every man in Kelly's Corner wasn't over in the booth with her. Jack shook his head. Eleanor was clearly on the prowl. She was wearing her low-cut tight red dress leaving little to the imagination.

As Jack walked back and set the beer on the bar, he cocked his head. "New to these parts?" he asked.

The young man looked a little annoyed, but the size of the beer seemed to mellow him a tad. "Just blowing through," he said. "Looking to see what this part of town has to offer."

"As in?"

The young man grinned. "Ladies."

Jack nodded. Just what he had figured. A predator.

"We have a few," Jack said and occupied himself with collecting empty bottles to send to recycle. "Doubt you will see any of them in here tonight, though."

The young man looked a little puzzled as he gestured towards Eleanor. "What about that hot chick in the corner."

"She's a cougar, son," Jack said and shook his head. "She's a little out of your league."

"What makes you say that?" the young man asked with a frown.

"I know her." Jack dumped the bottles into the bin and went back to cleaning glasses. Several regulars were starting to filter out, even though it was early. It was a chilly night, and many of them wanted to be home before the midnight hour because of the killings. Random spots around the city had reported women being murdered by a sick strangler who raped them as they died. The police were baffled because the killer was not sticking to one area, but moving randomly around the city and never being noticed no matter where the victim was found.

"So what's her name?" the young man asked a little too persistently. "And what's she drinking?"

Jack tried not to frown. He leaned his bulk over the bar and got a whiff of an odor he knew all too well. The scent of death was on this young man. Jack fought the urge to wrinkle his nose. "Her name is Eleanor, son, and as I said, she is a cougar. But if you must know, she likes a white wine spritzer."

"Make one and take it to her and tell her I sent it," the young man said, and he laid several large bills on the counter.

Jack sighed. *This won't end well,* he thought, but he went ahead and took the money and made the spritzer. He took it over to Eleanor who looked up and narrowed her eyes suspiciously at first. Her feline grace was unmistakable as she took the drink.

"From the young cub at the bar," Jack said.

Eleanor leaned appreciatively and held up the glass in a grateful salute. That was apparently all the invitation the young man needed. He practically dashed over and took the seat across from her.

"Hi," he said. "Name's Carson."

"Hi, Carson," Eleanor said, and her smile stretched in anticipation of the night to come.

Jack shook his head and lumbered back to the bar. He knew better than to stand between a predator and their prey.

He just hoped Eleanor would not make as much of a mess. It was getting harder to hose the bloodstains of her feasting off the bathroom walls...

END

Laura J. Underwood sometimes thinks she has been writing too long. Well, not really because as long as ideas are coming and people keep buying her books, she will keep on writing.

She is still an active member of SFWA and a former state fencing champion who sold her first piece of writing when she was seventeen. For over forty years since, she has been selling her nonfiction, short fiction and novels to various magazines, anthologies and publishers. Recent publications include *Tales from Keltora*, book two of the *Ard Magister* series *Demon In The Bones*, a novella titled *The Green Women*, and an electronic novella titled *The Hag Of The Wind*. Yard Dog Press will soon be releasing more adventures of her Keltoran characters, and she is actually working on a sequel to her Demon-Bound Duology (*Dragon's Tongue* and *Wandering Lark*). A native of East Tennessee, she works for a public library, collects ball jointed dolls based on her own characters, plays harp, makes bead dragons, occasionally draws and paints and knits and sews, and does whatever else she can in her precious spare time.

Aide De Tramp
Mel. White

The problem with losing your lizard, Old God Coyote decided, was that it left no one but yourself to talk with. Things had gotten complicated since the Pale People arrived and the First People started dying. Most of the Old Ones left to walk among the stars but Bear and Coyote stayed, listening to the gossip of the Little People—lizards and ants—that lived among the humans. But Yaxha, the lizard spirit who sang to him, had gone and now there was no one to talk with about this First Noble Deed of Coyotes.

He sat in the dust and waited for the woman and her mule to come walking by.

Just fifty more steps, Mariah Grant thought to herself. Fifty more and then she'd rest and check Jasper's hoof again. The mule wasn't limping as badly now, but her own feet were beginning to feel numb.

"Any minute now, Jasper... and there'll be a town ahead, just like the man said," she told the tired mule.

"Actually, Jud Greyson is a notoriously bad judge of distance," a voice said conversationally. "The town's about twenty minutes away."

Mariah jerked around. A scruffy coyote sat in the road behind her, a piece of marble balanced on its head.

"Now, I know what you're thinking..." the coyote began.

Mariah shrieked, "SATAN!" and scrambled into the saddle, flailing the reins. The mule bolted down the road.

"Well, that went rather well," the stone said sardonically.

"Give me time," Coyote said. "I just started helping her. At least this way she'll make town before supper."

"Nobody worships gods that scare people from one town to another as a form of rapid transportation. It's just further proof that people have forgotten you. You'll petrify before sundown, just like me, and humans will come and make statues of Jesus out of you."

Coyote's ears flattened. "Won't happen."

"Forgotten gods and rocks don't have a say in their fate. Are your toes feeling numb yet?"

"No." His paw kicked a pebble and it rattled into the grass.

"Liar. You're finding it harder to walk."

Coyote snorted. "Not true. I'm accident prone." He mentally sent an apology to the pebble, just in case it was the spirit of a lost god. "I'm just sorry I won't get to teach her about the Coyote magic I gave her."

"You gave a human magic? Is your head made of mud? Humans are impulsive and neglectful. Gods are the rightful holders of magic."

"The First People are proud. We don't go messing with their lives. We give them magic so they can solve their own problems.

"What a lazy bunch of deities. What magic did you give her?"

"Coyote magic is the magic of being clever and telling good stories."

"Being clever? Telling stories? No wonder no one believes in you. You'd have a lot more believers if you started striking them with thunderbolts."

"But—won't they be dead!"

"Of course. But the onlookers become very devout and devoted to pleasing you."

Jasper the mule stood still, his sweat-soaked sides heaving as Mariah began rubbing him down with a strip of sacking. She'd already lost friends, money, and more on her journey back to New York. She couldn't afford to lose the mule—not in this lost and lonely place of tall dry grass with only a bird circling in the cloudless sky for company.

There was a small shape in the distance—the coyote was slowly following her down the road. She wasn't sure if the animal was rabid or if the heat and sun had affected her mind, but it seemed safest to take no chances. Taking her brother's old pistol from the saddlebag, she carefully aimed at the animal. Legend said that silver bullets destroyed evil things. Lead bullets might only inconvenience them, but she cocked the hammer anyway.

The coyote sat down, tucking its tail neatly around its haunches.

"Death by gunshot. That might work. It would be fast, at any rate," the voice, acidic and feminine with a trace of an accent, seemed to come from the rock balanced on the creature's head.

The coyote sighed. "I'm feeling kind of reluctant to being shot."

"You said you might not be able to make it to the canyon to throw yourself off. Shooting you would be quick."

"But it will hurt."

"Slay him, woman," the rock said. "It's what he really wants."

"Don't rush her!"

Mariah steadied her aim. "Who... are you?"

"We're gods." The canine tilted his head and let the rock tumble to the ground. "I am Coyote and I am... I was... one of the Great Spirits of this land before your people came. My lizard said I was fading and said I should quit being lazy. I went to help the First People, but Bear told me to run off and growled at me. Tried helping a writer, but that turned out peculiar. So I looked around and saw you and your cloud of troubles and touched you with my magic. Then my lizard left me and I'm turning into rock so I'm not gonna be much help."

The odd turn of the conversation left her groping for words. "Your... lizard?"

"Lizards are singers who live among the people," he said as if it should be obvious even to the most feeble-minded. "They tell us gods what's happening in the world."

"And the talking rock?"

"She's not really a stone. She's a goddess—Aite. She's from Europe."

"Does she have lizards, too?"

The air went suddenly still and there was a slight smell of ozone. "You don't have much of an education." The goddess' tone was scathing.

Shame burned Mariah's cheeks. "I quit school at third grade."

"I suppose that's the best your Jesus can do," Aite sneered.

Mariah bridled. "That may be, but I'm not worshiping you," she snapped.

"You wouldn't suit me anyway. I am not a divinity of commoners." The ozone smell hung in the air. "My worshipers built temples of white marble for me in Troy."

Memory rose like an ancient whale rising towards a boat.

"A Trojan goddess?" Mariah couldn't recall the details but remembered thinking that the Greeks and Trojans fought a lot and their gods were awfully tetchy.

"I am the eldest daughter of Zeus and Eris."

Coyote sighed. "I wasn't exactly worshipped. I was more like a bad example. I died lots."

"Are you dying now?"

Aite's tone dripped acid "We both are. When a religion dies, its gods petrify. Your Jesus-god is taking away belief in other gods. After Mercury turned into a column of marble, I flew here to warn others. As I swooped down to talk to this flea-ridden deity, I turned into stone in mid-air. Almost hit him on the head and killed him."

"Ever since she warned me, I've been looking to find a place to hide so that after I turn into a rock, people won't come along and turn me into statues of Jesus because that would be insulting," Coyote added.

Silence stretched between them.

"Err... insulting to Jesus," he added quickly.

"So if you slay him, you'll be doing him a favor."

Mariah lowered the heavy gun and flexed her fingers. "You seem awfully eager to get rid of a fellow god."

"Too eager, yes," a voice at her feet observed. Mariah looked down. A fat brown lizard was sitting between her boots.

"Yaxha!" Coyote was on his feet, tail wagging enthusiastically.

"Your reptile, I presume?" The goddess' tone was disdainful.

"I am the one who sings to Coyote," the lizard said softly. "The wind whispered that we have a story of two gods who are no longer loved. It will make a good song."

"I doubt he was ever loved," Aiete sneered. "He wasn't much of a god in the first place."

Coyote hung his head. "Been awhile since I created things. Mostly the First People just tell stories about my bad manners and worse accidents."

"So nothing will be lost when you petrify," Aiete sounded as if she were smirking. "You won't be missed."

Yaxha padded over to the rock. Mariah had the impression that somewhere on a cosmic scale, a stare-down was going on. "An interesting situation, human," she said. "The wind says this goddess is the daughter of the Thunderer and Chaos and her true name is Misfortune. The only accident was that she did not land on his head and kill him."

"He wasn't much of a god to start with. I can take his place. Anything that he does, I can do better."

"So the tale begins when Coyote carries Misfortune to safety. But Misfortune wants his death." Yaxha tilted her head and looked at Mariah. "You must tell us how this is supposed to end."

"Me?"

"Who better to choose what happens? Coyote is only a little nobody of a god but he gave you a gift of stories to help you. You and he are much alike, struck by Misfortune. Humans have always told legends about gods. We do not have time to walk the road and find two others to pass judgement. You must finish this story. We will wait."

There was a slight emphasis on the word, 'story', as though the lizard was giving her a hint. Mariah frantically reviewed fairy tales from her childhood, but none seemed to fit the situation. No one was handing out poisoned apples, and Coyote was no enchanted prince. Frustration was making her headache worse. The three watched her, waiting with the patience of beings to whom a billion years was merely an afternoon nap. She felt trapped.

...trapped...

Memory stirred.

"Yes," she said as she carefully tore a strip from the sacking she'd used on the mule. "Let me see if I have this right. Gods everywhere are dying because nobody's worshiping them." She picked up the stone with her cloth-covered hand. "Aite wants to find people who are looking for bad things to happen to others. Coyote, here, is one of those bad luck gods and when she saw Coyote, turned into a rock so she could fall on his head and kill him."

"Badly put. He was going to die, anyway."

"But he did her a favor and picked her up and carried her off the road so she wouldn't be crushed by wagon wheels."

Coyote's ears drooped. "My last good deed in the world."

"It's like the tale of the man who let a tiger out of a trap," Mariah kept her tone casual as she drew the ends of the cloth together. "The ungrateful tiger wanted to eat him. He asked a jackal to be the judge and the jackal said they should go back to the place where the story started."

"That's so insightful," Aiete sneered.

Yaxha winked.

"Well, this story started with you falling out of the sky." Mariah whirled the improvised sling and threw the stony goddess upward and outward as hard as she could. "Now, Coyote, you can choose between running out there and stand where she can kill you with her fall, or you can go do something else."

Coyote sat beside her, tail tucked around his haunches. "Good arm, there," he observed. "Ever think about going into that new-fangled sport of baseball?"

"I'm going home back to where my story started," she said. "Colorado's a new state and it needs a different kind of person. New York's really my home."

"I suppose I could come along and help you." He smiled up at her; tongue lolling between his sharp white teeth.

Mariah set her foot in the stirrup and grinned back. "We've got Boss Tweed in City Hall. I don't think New York needs more scoundrels. Besides, there's bound to be someone else around here who needs a bit of Coyote magic." She clucked to the mule and headed him toward town.

And Great God Coyote looked back towards the place where Aiete fell. "I know a nice canyon where no one could find Misfortune," he said thoughtfully.

"You were going to start helping humans," Yaxha reminded him as she scrambled onto his tail. "Do not worry about forgotten gods. Worry about the world instead."

He examined his toes and found that they weren't stone after all. Then he gathered his haunches and leaped high into the sky. "The town she left behind her doesn't have a library. How will they ever know Coyote stories if there's no library?"

"But the books they get may have stories about Aiete," Yaxha reminded him.

"Not to worry," Coyote said. "I'm taking a personal interest in the mail, too."

Mel White was adopted into a tribe of Coyotes at a very early age and spent most of her childhood practicing to become Very Peculiar. She recently retired from her long career as the Dread Space Pirate Inuwei Seregon, and has now settled into the role of Minecraft and Warcraft addict. Her hobbies include arguing with people on Internet and collecting academic degrees.

About the Cover Artists

Sherri Dean was born late AND backwards in a small town in Missouri, which explains a lot, her mundane hours are spent as a veteran of the animal health field (and the recipient of many a puppy piddling) until she gets rich and famous. Or was that infamous? She spends her quality time writing, illustrating, making crazy costumes and reading.

She credits Forrest J "Uncle Forry" Ackerman for her love of Science Fiction, fantasy and horror, and is active in genre conventions throughout the Midwest. It is at one of these early conventions she encountered the infamous (there's that word again! Buy a thesaurus already!) Selina "BUY MY BOOKS!" Rosen and was thusly corrupted to submit cover art, stories and mad editing skills for Yard Dog Press. Sherri's latest works available are the Weird Western collection with co-author Bill D. Allen titled *Three Aces from Satan's Hand* and the horror anthology *Death is Only Skin Deep* with Tim W. Burke and Allison Stein. Both are available online, so get crackin' as they won't last long!

Sherri has long referred to herself in the third person, the "royal we," if you will, as the Queen of the Flying Monkeys for years and has recently earned the title of The Feisty Mistress of Fear. (If you've met her you already know. If not, do so and BUY HER STUFF!) In addition to commanding her monkey minions she likes shiny presents and hearing from fans on Facebook, Twitter and the upcoming website. Now, go forth and make with the monkey adoration! She needs praise; lie if you must.

James Hollaman has stories in three of the *Bubbas of the Apocalypse* anthologies—*International House of Bubbas*, *Houston We've Got Bubbas!*, and *A Bubba In Time Saves None*. He also has a story in *Flush Fiction I*, and *I Didn't Quite Make It To Oz*.

Jimmy did the cover art for *The Bubba Chronicles*, *Marking the Signs and Other Tales of Mischief*, and *I Didn't Quite Make*

It To Oz in addition to the art on the back cover of this volume. He is always creating.

He also runs a "small" convention party called Room Con.

Yard Dog Press Titles As Of This Print Date

The Guardians, Lynn Abbey
Hammer Town, Selina Rosen
The Happiness Box, Beverly A. Hale
The Host Series: The Host, Fright Eater, Gang Approval, Selina
    Rosen
Houston, We've Got Bubbas!, Edited by Selina Rosen
How I Spent the Apocolypse, Selina Rosen
I Didn't Quite Make It To Oz, Edited by Selina Rosen
I Should Have Stayed In Oz, Edited by Selina Rosen
In the Shadows, Bradley H. Sinor
International House of Bubbas, Edited by Selina Rosen
It's the Great Bumpkin, Cletus Brown!, Katherine A. Turski
The Killswitch Review, Steven-Elliot Altman & Diane DeKelb-
    Rittenhouse
The Leopard's Daughter, Lee Killough
The Lightning Horse, John Moore
The Logic of Departure, Mark W. Tiedemann
The Long, Cold Walk To Mars, Jeffrey Turner
Marking the Signs and Other Tales Of Mischief, Laura J.
    Underwood
Material Things, Selina Rosen
Medieval Misfits: Renaissance Rejects, Tracy S. Morris
Mirror Images, Susan Satterfield
Mirror, Mirror and Other Reflections, James K. Burk
More Stories That Won't Make Your Parents Hurl, Edited by
    Selina Rosen
Music for Four Hands, Louis Antonelli & Edward Morris
My Life with Geeks and Freaks, Claudia Christian
The Necronomicrap: A Guide To Your Horooscope, Tim Frayser
Playing With Secrets, Bradley H & Sue P. Sinor
Redheads In Love, Linda L. Donahue, Rhonda Eudaly, Julia S.
    Mandala, & Dusty Rainbolt
Reruns, Selina Rosen
Rock 'n' Roll Universe, Ken Rand
Shadows In Green, Richard Dansky
Stories That Won't Make Your Parents Hurl, Edited by Selina
    Rosen
Tales from Keltora, Laura J. Underwood
Tales Of the Lucky Nickel Saloon, Second Ave., Laramie,
    Wyoming, U S of A, Ken Rand
Tarbox Station, Rhonda Eudaly
Texistani: Indo-Pak Food From A Texas Kitchen, Beverly A. Hale
That's All Folks, J. F. Gonzalez
Through Wyoming Eyes, Ken Rand
Turn Left to Tomorrow, Robin Wayne Bailey
The Twins, Selina Rosen

Wandering Lark, Laura J. Underwood
Wings of Morning, Katharine Eliska Kimbriel
Zombies In Oz and Other Undead Musings, Robin Wayne Bailey

Double Dog
(A YDP Imprint):

#1:
Of Stars & Shadows, Mark W. Tiedemann
This Instance Of Me, Jeffrey Turner

#2:
Gods and Other Children, Bill D. Allen
Tranquility, Tracy Morris

#3:
Home Is the Hunter, James K. Burk
Farstep Station, Lazette Gifford

#4:
Sabre Dance, Melanie Fletcher
The Lunari Mask, Laura J. Underwood

#5:
House of Doors, Julia Mandala
Jaguar Moon, Linda A. Donahue

Just Cause
(A YDP Imprint):

The Bitter End
Selina Rosen

Death Under the Crescent Moon
Dusty Rainbolt

The Ghost Writer
Selina Rosen

It's Not Rocket Science: Spirituality for the Working-Class Soul
Selina Rosen

Meditations of a Hoarder
Melinda LaFevers

Not My Life
Selina Rosen

The Pit
Selina Rosen

Plots and Protagonists: A Reference Guide for Writers
Mel. White

Vanishing Fame
Selina Rosen

Non-YDP titles we distribute:

Chains of Freedom
Chains of Destruction
Jabone's Sword
Queen of Denial
Recycled
Strange Robby
Sword Masters
Selina Rosen

Three Ways to Order:

1. Write us a letter telling us what you want, then send it along with your check or money order (made payable to Yard Dog Press) to: Yard Dog Press, 710 W. Redbud Lane, Alma, AR 72921-7247

2. Use selinarosen@cox.net or lynnstran@cox.net to contact us and place your order. Then send your check or money order to the address above. *This has the advantage of allowing you to check on the availability of short-stock items such as T-shirts and back-issues of Yard Dog Comics.*

3. Contact us as in #1 or #2 above and pay with a credit card or by debit from your checking account. Either give us the credit card information in your letter/Email/phone call, or go to our website and use our shopping carts. If you send us your information, please include your name as it appears on the card, your credit card number, the expiration date, and the 3 or 4-digit security code after your signature on the back (CVV). Please remember that we will include media rate (minimum $3.00) S/H for mailing in the lower 48 states.

Watch our website at
www.yarddogpress.com
for news of upcoming projects
and new titles!!

A Note to Our Readers

We at Yard Dog Press understand that many people buy used books because they simply can't afford new ones. That said, and understanding that not everyone is made of money, we'd like you to know something that you may not have realized. Writers only make money on new books that sell. At the big houses a writer's entire future can hinge on the number of books they sell. While this isn't the case at Yard Dog Press, the honest truth is that when you sell or trade your book or let many people read it, the writer and the publishing house aren't making any money.

As much as we'd all like to believe that we can exist on love and sweet potato pie, the truth is we all need money to buy the things essential to our daily lives. Writers and publishers are no different.

We realize that these "freebies" and cheap books often turn people on to new writers and books that they wouldn't otherwise read. However we hope that you will reconsider selling your copy, and that if you trade it or let your friends borrow it, you also pass on the information that if they really like the author's work they should consider buying one of their books at full price sometime so that the writer can afford to continue to write work that entertains you.

We appreciate all our readers and *depend* upon their support.

Thanks,
The Editorial Staff
Yard Dog Press

PS – Please note that "used" books without covers have, in most cases, been stolen. Neither the author nor the publisher has made any money on these books because they were supposed to be pulped for lack of sales.

Please do not purchase books without covers.

www.ingramcontent.com/pod-product-compliance
Lightning Source LLC
Chambersburg PA
CBHW020643250626
47154CB00008B/2793